Kernowland

Pigleg's Revenge

Book Four

Titles available in the Kernowland series:

Kernowland

Pigleg's Revenge

Jack Trelawny

The Chronicles of
ERTHWURLD

CAMPION BOOKS

A catalogue record for this book
is available from the British Library

ISBN 978-0-9546338-7-5

Campion Books is an Imprint of Campion Publishing Limited

Illustrations by Louise Hackman-Hexter

Printed in the UK by CPI William Clowes
Beccles NR34 7TL

First published in the UK in 2008 by

CAMPION BOOKS
2 Lea Valley House
Stoney Bridge Drive
Waltham Abbey
Essex, UK
EN9 3LY

www.kernowland.com
www.erthwurld.com

For Tizzie and Louis

AUTHOR'S  NOTES

Apart from Tizzie & Louis,
the characters and events in this book
are entirely fictitious.

In the *Erthwurld* books,
'Erth' means 'Earth',
and 'Wurld' means 'World'.
Evile is pronounced *ee-vile* to rhyme with mile.
Skotos is pronounced *skoh-toss* – it means 'darkness' in Greek.
Photos is pronounced *foh-toss* – it means 'of light' in Greek.
Graph means 'draw' in Greek, so a *photograph* is…
'a picture drawn with light'.

Websites
There is lots of other information
as well as clickable zooming maps
on the Kernowland and Erthwurld websites

www.kernowland.com
www.erthwurld.com

ONE

Party Island

The Revenger sailed on, making good progress with the wind pushing and the whalehorses pulling.

It was midday.

The sun blazed angrily in the sky.

A cluster of seven volcanic islands loomed on the horizon as they travelled south.

'The Isles of Airanac!' bellowed Captain Pigleg.

'We'll soon be at Airanac Narg, shipmates,' yelled Mr Cudgel.

'Party Island!' roared the crew in unison.

'Yay… 'tiz that to be sure,' said Pigleg, with a rare smile, 'an' me favourite lady's waitin' fer me there.'

Erthwurld's most feared and fearsome pirate was excited.

He hadn't seen his girlfriend, Big Bessie, for a very long time.

'YAYYY!' cheered the crew.

They were all excited about seeing their wives and girl-friends too.

It was the last chance they'd get before *the hunt*…

For Big… Red… Grunter.

They all knew that some of them would not return from the perilous voyage to Jungleland.

So they were planning to make it a party to remember.

The ship made straight for the island's capital, Samlap Sal.

Pigleg and his men could do as they pleased in this place. There was no law of any kind on these wild and remote isles.

7

Down in the hold of the ship, Tizzie was listening to all the noise on deck.

It made her wonder what was happening to cause so much excitement amongst the pirates.

And what would it mean for her?

Then her worry-thoughts returned to her constant concern.

Where was Louis?

Would she ever see her little brother again?

Was he even alive?

TWO

The Desert Of Arahas

The desert seemed endless. A vast ocean of sand swept away from them in every direction.

Louis' head and face were covered to protect him from the searing heat and the skin-scraping storms. Akbar had given him a desert robe to wear over his uniform, and he was very thankful for it.

'I will teach you both all I can about survival in the desert,' the warrior sheik had said as they set out on their long journey. 'The more you know, the more chance you have of surviving long enough to reach Jungleland. Especially if we get separated.'

Louis had therefore resolved to watch, listen, and learn everything he could from Akbar, so that, whatever happened, he had the best possible chance of rescuing his sister.

The first day in the Desert of Arahas had been just as the young boy had imagined it would be. Sandy. Dry. Hot.

The first *night* had not been at all as he had imagined. Cold. Freezing, in fact. The second night was the same. He was certainly glad of the warmth afforded by the robe.

Day three, today, was particularly hot. Louis felt as if someone had turned up the temperature dial on the oven they were cooking in.

The exhausted young boy was doing a mental check that he had everything he needed with him. He had rolled up his cape and packed it away, along with the jacket of his uniform, in a saddle bag. It was far too hot to wear either of them under his desert robe. *Zoomer* was safely inside its case, rolled in his cape.

9

He was wearing his Kaski, catapult, and cataball ammo belt under the robe. The old, tattered parchment map of Kernowland was folded in the inside pocket of his black shirt. His Kernow compass was still hanging around his neck. And, perhaps most importantly, the Golden Key was still safe in his trouser pocket.

Akbar had shown him how to ride a quadcamel. The sheik had called the giant animal, 'the ship of the desert'.

Louis sat behind his teacher, between the second and third humps of the huge camel. He was sitting as he had been told, but it was proving harder than it looked to get comfortable.

As he, Akbar, and Hans travelled onwards on the two quadcamels, Louis' legs and bottom had become very sore from the constant swaying movement.

'I should tell you we are seeking the Blue Turbans,' said Akbar. 'They are a tribe of very fierce desert warriors, so called because they wear headscarves dyed with indigo. Like my people, they are rebels and they fight the Empire whenever and wherever they can. They are in constant contact with members of RAE in Jungleland. They will know who we should contact to get help in rescuing your sister. And they will have messenger birds, so we can send details of our mission ahead to the rebels in the jungle.'

This was a lot for Louis to take in but he tried to commit everything Akbar told him to memory. It could be important.

As they trudged on and on through the searing heat and shifting sands, Louis tried to think of anything other than his sore bottom.

His mind kept wandering between three thoughts.

How were three of them going to rescue Tizzie from a whole shipload of pirates?

Was there *any* chance that his friend Mr Sand had survived?

And what had happened to Misty, the little blue mouse?

THREE

ESCAPED!

'ESCAPED!' screamed Manaccan the Merciless at the top of his voice.

His new subjects were learning quickly that he had a terrible, terrible temper.

The Chief Guard confirmed the news as he bowed his head before his King in the empty dungeon.

'Yes, Your Majesticness. It's like they just disappeared into thin…'

'Enough of your excuses!

'The Guillotine of Sirap is on its way here. I'm going to lop off plenty of heads when that big razor arrives – and you'll be first if you say another word. Now get out of my sight.'

The Chief Guard looked visibly relieved that he would be keeping his head as he backed out of the dungeon and hurried away down the corridor as fast as he could go.

'Lister.'

'Yes, my King,' said the Counterupper, who was standing at the dungeon doorway, meticulously recording everything as usual.

'Get reward posters done straight away, and send them around the Empire by messenger bird.'

'We've already printed some posters of Prince Louis and put them up around Kernowland, sire.'

'Yes I know that, but now we need four new posters.

'The boy prince…

'My cousin, Kea...

'Sand…

'And that infernal, interfering gnome.

'I want *big* rewards offered for them all…

'Clearly marked on the posters.

'Put five hundred evos on each of their heads.

'Dead or alive.'

'Yes, my King.'

'Better still… make it five *thousand* evos for the Prince.

'That'll mean every rogue and bounty hunter in Erthwurld will be after him.'

FOUR

Megan's Medicine

Dark green mermaid blood stained the pool inside the cave as Megan the mermaid was brought to the surface of the water.

Morwenna had dived in to rescue her.

'Look, her tail's been bitten off,' she said to the others, pointing a trembling finger at the oozing wound as she did so.

All the mermaids stared at their injured friend.

'Is she unconscious?' asked Mylene.

'Yes,' answered Morwenna.

'Thank goodness for that,' said Mylene. 'When she wakes up… that's going to hurt.'

'We must gather lots of blue-green seaweed to stop the bleeding and help the healing,' said Morwenna. 'Someone will have to go out of the cave and see if the killerwhales have gone.'

As soon as she had spoken, Morwenna could see from their reactions that her friends were hesitating. With Megan incapacitated and needing urgent help, it had become obvious that she would have to take charge and take action.

'You look after her as best you can until I get back.'

Without further delay, she dived into the pool.

Deep below the surface, Morwenna looked through the hole in the rock. She couldn't be sure if the whales had gone.

Now she had a dilemma.

If she put her head through the hole and Kracka or Kruncha was on the other side, she would be decapitated.

Tails could grow back. Heads couldn't!

But Morwenna knew that her friend only had a couple of hours at most to live. If Megan didn't get the blue-green seaweed packed on her wound very soon… she would die.

There really was *no choice*.

Morwenna knew she could only save her friend's life by risking her own. She summoned all her courage… and put her head through the hole.

No crack. No crunch.

She swam through.

Still nothing.

Phew! The killerwhales seemed to have gone.

She went back into the cave and told the others that the coast was clear. There was no time to lose.

'Mylene, you stay here and look after Megan. The rest of us need to swim as fast as we can and bring back as much blue-green seaweed as we are able to carry.'

The five mermaids fanned out and swam as fast as they could to the nearest places they could gather the blue-green seaweed.

In no time at all they each had a large clump of it clutched in their arms, and they each flipped their tails extra quickly as they sped back to the pool cave.

Morwenna and Mylene made a medicinal drink with some of the seaweed, to help Megan's pain, whilst the other mermaids packed the rest of the healing plant around the injury.

'We'll need to give her the medicine and put fresh seaweed dressings on the wound for seven days,' said Morwenna. 'That will keep it clean while it starts to grow back.'

'So will she be okay?' asked Maria.

'My grandmother lost her tail in a shark attack,' said Melanie.

'Her friends did the same thing for her. Mother said it only took about a month or so to grow back.'

All the other mermaids knew the story of Melanie's grandmother losing her tail and it growing back. But they still felt better for hearing it again.

They were all very thankful that they'd been able to get the seaweed in time.

They hoped and hoped that Megan would survive the attack by the killerwhales, and that her tail would grow back just like it was before.

FIVE

Serving Slaves

The Revenger arrived at the island of Airanac Narg in the late afternoon.

As the whalehorses pulled the ship into its dock in the harbour, Pigleg barked out his orders.

'Get some provisions for the party.'

Six pirates went off to the old part of the town with a bag of gold evos.

They came back later with a creaking old cartwagon drawn by two very sad and mangy-looking donkeygoats.

The party provisions were unloaded and hauled aboard.

There were kegs of rum and ale, bottles of wine and port, and boxes and bags of all kinds of food.

'The WAGs'll be 'ere soon, lads!' shouted Pigleg. 'And then we'll make this a party to remember!'

'YAYYY!' cheered the crew.

'Mr Cudgel, get them slavelings up 'ere a workin' for their keep.'

'Aye, aye, Cap'n.'

'Purgy, get the slaves on deck. Seven and older.'

'Just as you say, Mr Cudgel, just as you say.'

Tizzie watched Purgy come down the steps into the hold.

The tattoo-mouth smirked as he spoke.

'Some of you layabouts are needed on deck. There are some guests coming aboard who need looking after like the proper ladies that they are. Only seven-year-olds and over for this job. And the

Cap'n will have no talking. Just do as you're told… *when* you're told. Or there'll be trouble… real trouble.'

Tizzie – and all the other children who were the right age – ascended the steps into the dazzling brightness of the sun.

She squinted to protect her eyes.

'Right, line up by the rail,' said Purgy.

He then proceeded to hand them each a small folded cloth.

'You're going to be serving slaves, fetching and carrying food and drinks. And washing glasses and plates in this keg of sea water. The cloth is for drying. And you'd better do it properly… or else.'

Tizzie was worried she might not be any good at this job… as she'd never served or done any washing up before. And she wasn't sure her experience washing nappies in Sandland would help either.

Purgy then gave them some more instructions on how to be good serving slaves.

As she was listening to what she had to do, Tizzie noticed something unusual. Lots of the pirates had combed their hair. Others looked as if they might have even washed, because their faces and hands were clean.

A little while later, the reason for the sprucing-up became clear when the brightly-dressed wives and girlfriends of the pirates came stumbling along the dock.

Their clothes were a bit dishevelled. And they were all carrying half-empty bottles of wine, and singing strange songs, very loudly and very badly out of tune. It looked and sounded like they'd already begun the merrymaking elsewhere.

'YAYYY!'

The pirates cheered.

'Here come the WAGs!'

'There's my wife, Alice!' shouted one happy husband.

'Hello, Beth,' yelled another excited pirate as he waved to his girlfriend.

The women came aboard.

A wild and noisy party began.

About half-an-hour into her serving duty, Tizzie noticed that Captain Pigleg was still standing alone by the ship's wheel.

'Where's the Captain's girlfriend?' she whispered to Jack as he was passing with yet another tray of drinks balanced on his hand.

'Jenny said that Big Bessie is always late,' answered Jack. 'Apparently, as the most important WAG, she likes to make a grand entrance.'

'What's she like?'

'See for yourself. Look, over there...

'Here she comes now.'

SIX

I Want To Race

Bang!

'Yeeeyeeeyaaahhhhhh!'

Bang!

'Yeeeyeeeyaaahhhhhh!'

One baking afternoon, as he swayed along with the movement of the quadcamel, Louis was startled by the sound of yelling and gunfire beyond a range of huge sand dunes ahead.

A sand cloud was rising into the air from behind one of the dunes.

'If that's what I think it is, we're in for some fun,' said Akbar.

When they reached the brow of the sand dune, Akbar looked down and smiled.

'Just as I thought. Camel racing!'

Akbar led Louis and Hans down the other side of the dune.

As they approached a group of tents and awnings, the sheik issued a warning.

'These are the Blue Turbans I told you about. They are suspicious of all outsiders. Especially Whiteskins. Do not speak to them until I have introduced you.'

There were lots of camels herded together near the tents. Some of them were drinking from a long, rectangular, stone trough full of grey water. Louis thought the trough must be at least thirty paces long.

Akbar was soon talking to a group of men, some of whom he seemed to know.

He pointed now and then at Louis as the conversation continued.

The other men were laughing and joking and also pointing at Louis.

Akbar then walked back and spoke to Louis and Hans.

'When I asked them for help in rescuing your sister, Louis, they readily agreed. But when I told them more – that you were a warrior prince from Forestland, who could ride a pony like a grown man – they found something amusing in it.'

'Zat iss not nice, zey haven't seen him ride,' said Hans. 'He could be gut for all zey know.'

'That's what I told them,' said Akbar, 'but then they just kept making fun and laughing at the thought of Louis, a boy from Eporue, who has never raced a camel, taking part in a race against their own boys. The desert boys grow up on camels, you see, so they're used to riding and racing them. I said it would not be fair, as you've never done it before. Then they just said that you'd be too scared anyway, because you could easily fall off and be seriously injured or killed. And Sandland boys are braver than boys from Eporue.'

Louis wasn't sure he found any of that particularly correct... or *funny*.

Then Akbar leant forward and continued in a more serious tone.

'But that conversation was just an amusement. As I said before, the Blue Turbans are members of RAE. The main discussion was about sending a note by messenger bird to the rebels in Nwotegroeg in Jungleland.

'The leader of the rebels there is a woman who is fiercely loyal to the cause. Her whole family is involved in the fight against

Evile. If they are informed of our mission to rescue your sister, they'll discover where Tizzie is, so that it will be quicker to find her when we arrive.'

Louis and Hans nodded as Akbar spoke, to show that they thought it was a good plan.

'And, importantly, they'll assist in the rescue. We are only three against a whole shipload of pirates… and that's not good odds, even if we do have surprise on our side.'

'Well at least you don't have to race a camel,' said Hans, smiling down at Louis and patting him on the shoulder. 'Looks dangerous.'

'But I want to,' said Louis, defiantly.

In that moment, something had become very clear to him.

He just *knew* it was important that he play the role he had been given as best he could. He *had* to show these men that he *wasn't* a scared little boy.

Akbar looked at Louis as if considering something very important.

'But you've never raced before. It's difficult… and extremely dangerous. You could be killed. Are you *sure*?'

For all that he had just said, Akbar looked very pleased to hear Louis' loudly spoken answer.

'I am Prince Louis of Forestland.

'I want to race.'

SEVEN

Big Bessie

Big Bessie was called 'Big' for a reason.

She was *BIG* in every sense of the word.

She had a big body, a big voice, a big personality, and, everybody who knew her agreed, a great big kind heart.

Bessie was a Blackskin, from Sodabrab, one of the Neabbirac Islands, which lay just off the south-eastern coast of Acirema North.

She rolled along the dock towards the ship like a bundle of moving sound, hitching up her long skirts and petticoats as she waddle-hurried as fast as she could go.

'Where's my Little Piggyleggy, then?' she screamed over and over again at the top of her big voice.

'There's me big girl. Here at last!'

Captain Pigleg, from the twinkle in his eye, was very obviously delighted to see her.

'Piggyleggy! Piggyleggy! Piggyleggy!'

But he did seem a little uncomfortable that she was shouting out her nickname for him in front of all his men.

Bessie rolled aboard and made straight for Pigleg.

'Give me a hug, you naughty pirate, you,' she said, as her wobbling arms went around him in a suffocating bear-hug. 'Oooo. It's been too long apart again.'

'You!' shouted Pigleg, barely managing to point his golden hook at Tizzie from within Bessie's smothering grasp. 'Rum for me, and port for me favourite girl! And don't tarry neither!'

Tizzie hurried as fast as she could.

As she brought back the drinks on a tray, she couldn't help but overhear the conversation between the Captain and his girlfriend.

'But you know the rules, my big pumpkin dumplin'. Absolutely no WAGs allowed on board *The Revenger* when we're sailin'. Never... Not ever. It distracts the men from their work.'

'Oh, come on Piggy, just this once. My grandma in Nwotegroeg wants to see me. She's very old and poorly now, and it might be my last chance. Pleeeeease, Piggyleggy.'

Pigleg took a glug from his tankard, and was deep in thought for a few moments before he made his decision.

'Aye, okay then. You can come with us to Jungleland. But just this once... Agreed?'

'Oh yes, thank you so much, my lovely pirate,' she said before planting a big squelchy kiss on her boyfriend's cheek.

The news travelled around the ship in no time at all. When they learned of Pigleg's decision, the other WAGs murmured and whispered amongst themselves. They were more than a little upset that Big Bessie was getting special treatment... *again*. But neither they nor their men dared say so in case the Captain heard them and got angry. Everybody in Erthwurld knew it was *not* a good idea to rile Cap'n Pigleg, the most fearsome pirate who had ever lived.

After a while, everyone seemed to forget about Big Bessie being allowed to sail on the ship to Jungleland, and they all went back to having a wild time.

'Get them young'uns below,' shouted Pigleg at some time well after midnight. 'We'll serve ourselves from now on.'

'Right yoou lott, get beloow,' slurred Purgy, who, like all the pirates and WAGs, seemed to have had a little too much to drink.

The children did as they were told. Tizzie was exhausted as she finally descended the steps into the hold. Within minutes of her head hitting her rag pillow, she was fast asleep.

* * *

Next morning, the children were rudely awoken by Purgy shouting down into the hold.

'Get up on deck, now. There's lots of cleaning and clearing-up work to do.'

Tizzie rubbed her eyes. It was hard to wake up this morning as she'd had a late night. On deck, she was soon feeling the heat of the sun on her back as she tidied and cleaned.

The ship was strewn with snoring bodies, broken bottles, half-eaten pigchicken drumsticks, lumps of geeps cheese, chewed cobs of cornwheat, and all manner of other party left-overs.

Later in the day, just as Tizzie and the others were finishing the cleaning up, there was frantic activity amongst the pirates. Supplies were being brought aboard for the next leg of the sea journey to Jungleland.

Pigleg had kept to his promise, and Big Bessie was aboard *The Revenger* as the pirate ship sailed out of the harbour of Samlap Sal. But, because the Captain's girlfriend had agreed not to distract the men from their duties, she stayed in her cabin and slept. Sleeping was something she did an awful lot of anyway.

Tizzie was worrying about Louis as she scrubbed the last dish clean. But her thoughts quickly returned to the imminent encounter with Big Red Grunter as the Captain bellowed out his orders.

'Get those steeds a-pullin' for Jungleland...

'We're going on a *pig hunt*!'

EIGHT

Dead Or Alive?

Pemberley the butler was spying.

He had been watching everything that went on in the castle, using his network of secret corridors and peepholes.

At this particular moment, he was watching Mr Lister at work through one of the peepholes.

The King's Counterupper was drawing four separate posters. Each had a different picture on it.

Princess Kea, Mr Sand, Clevercloggs… and Prince Louis.

There was an offer of a reward written on them.

Five hundred evos for three of the outlaws.

And five *thousand* evos for the young prince.

But most worrying were the words at the bottom…

Dead or Alive!

Pemberley went to the kitchen and expressed his concerns to Mrs Portwrinkle, who was very wise in the ways of the wurld and generally had good, sound advice to offer.

'You're close to the King,' she said. 'You see him all the time. We can use that to our advantage. We need to make him think you're on his side. And then we've got to get him to do what we want.

'The most important thing is to get those reward posters changed to something less dangerous before they're sent out to all the far-flung corners of the Empire. It was one thing when they were looking for him in Kernowland, but it's quite another if the search is going to be widened. There are some very nasty bounty hunters out there in Erthwurld. If they'd still get the reward, most of them would think nothing of killing someone who's wanted rather than capturing them alive. It saves feeding the prisoners on the way back here.'

Pemberley agreed with everything Mrs Portwrinkle had said.

'Yes, that's true. Princess Kea and the others will have a much better chance of being brought back to Kernowland still breathing if we can get the *dead* word removed from the posters.'

The cook and the butler began to hatch a plan.

* * *

Mrs Portwrinkle made Mr Lister a nice cup of tea. Just the way he liked it. With lots of milk and six heaped spoonfuls of sugar.

Pemberley then visited Lister's office with the tea, and took a special interest in the posters.

Next morning, the butler was helping Manaccan the Merciless to get dressed.

Alone with the King, he seized his chance.

'Your Majesty, I hope you don't mind my saying, but I was fortunate enough to see Mr Lister preparing the 'Wanted' posters for Prince Louis and the other criminals.'

'Yes, Pemberley. With rewards like that on offer to the bounty hunters of Erthwurld, I'm sure we'll have four heads on stakes at the castle gates before the Emperor arrives in Kernowland.'

'Indeed, sire. And those villains jolly well deserve all they get too. But… could I suggest that perhaps it would be better to bring them all back alive?'

'How so?'

'If they are brought here *alive*, there could be a *fair trial*, sire. That way, you could show your commitment to the rule of law and fair play for all. Even suspected traitors. The people would think that you are fair and just. And support you.'

'I don't need anyone's support. I'm the King!'

'Yes, indeed you are, sire. But it might perhaps make your job easier if you are seen to be a fair-minded ruler. And the people will *love* you all the more for it.'

From the look on Manaccan's face, Pemberley could see he'd hit one of the King's soft buttons. Although he said he didn't care, it was apparent that, deep down, Manaccan the Merciless rather liked the idea of the people liking him.

The butler saw the moment was right to use what he had seen and overheard through the secret peephole in the Throne Room.

'And then, when the criminals are convicted, there could be a *public execution* to demonstrate what will happen to anyone who gets in your way.'

Manaccan looked at his butler out of the corner of his eye.

'That's uncanny, Pemberley. I seem to remember saying something very similar myself, not so long ago. I think we'll have to keep having these little chats.'

'Of course, sire...

'Anything for my King.'

NINE

Barq The Chargercamel

'Now remember this is a chargercamel,' warned Akbar as he helped Louis get ready for the race and showed him what to do.

'His name is Barq, which means *lightning* in our language. He's specially bred for racing. He can run very fast but the ride will be difficult and dangerous. As you see, just one hump, which makes balancing hard. He'll bounce you all over the place and, if you fall, you could be trampled and killed.'

Louis had already begun to have second thoughts about the race before Akbar had started talking. Now, as the sheik continued, he was definitely concerned that he may have made the wrong decision.

'This special forked horn saddle helps. It's called a tamzak. It goes in front of the hump, on these two cloths. Then you sit on it like this. And put your legs on the camel's neck. That helps you tell him which direction to go. But it makes balancing even harder, so you'll have to grip tightly with your legs, like this. Then you hold the reins like this.'

Suddenly, as Louis was trying to take it all in, a voice spoke inside Louis' head.

'*Why do I always get the beginners?*'

This made him respond without thinking.

'I may be a beginner, but I always try my best.'

Louis was talking to the camel, but Akbar thought the comment was made to him.

'I'm sure you will, little warrior, I'm sure you will.'

'*Hmmm, good attitude,*' said the thought voice. '*I'll try my best too then.*'

Louis was very glad to hear it and his concerns were somewhat alleviated as Akbar took Barq's bit in his hand and began leading the camel and rider towards the starting line.

'Now, a little bit of advice which may help you,' said the sheik quietly. 'Sometimes we can achieve more by doing less. By *letting go* of what we think is our control over things.'

Louis nodded to show he was listening as Akbar continued.

'My friends told me this is a very, very fast camel. When the race starts, just let him run. Most boys, even the sons of the desert, let fear enter their hearts. So they hold on too tightly to the reins... and slow their camel down. But, if you just let him go, Barq will run like the wind. Put all fearful thoughts of falling far from your mind. Let go! Then you can triumph!'

Louis could see in Akbar's eyes, and hear in his voice, that he considered this to be important advice. The kind sheik wasn't just coaching Louis to finish the race. He thought he could *win*.

'I understand,' answered Louis, 'just let him run.'

'Yes! little warrior. Conquer your fear, and let go. Then you can achieve more than you ever dreamed.'

Beyond the tents, a racetrack was marked out by two lines of ropes, supported, at regular intervals, by wooden posts.

About a dozen camels were lined up at the start line.

Boy jockeys, all about his own age as far as Louis could make out, sat on their saddles and held the reins of each camel. They were obviously just about to start the race. Louis joined them, his heart beating fast.

Just as he arrived at the start line, there was a very loud noise as a pistol shot rang out.

Bang! And they were off!

Barq shot away from the start like a bullet from a gun.

'Whoaaah!'

Louis bobbled and bounced all over the place on the back of the chargercamel as it raced down the track.

The terrified young boy's natural reaction was to pull on the reins. He gripped tightly and tugged.

Some of the other boys did the same.

Barq slowed down.

'*Oh no, he's a scared one,*' said the voice in Louis' head.

On hearing this, Louis remembered Akbar's words.

'Conquer your fear... let go...'

Louis gripped the tamzak tightly with his legs, let go of the reins, leant back in the saddle, closed his eyes, and put his arms out to the side.

'Run Barq... RUN!'

'*That's more like it... A Warrior Heart.*'

As Louis heard the words in his head, he felt Barq surge forward beneath him. Then the chargercamel extended his neck and quickened his gallop still further.

Louis gripped tighter with his legs. He heard some of the Blue Turbans in the crowd shouting loudly.

'It's Prince Louis!'

'He's taking the lead.'

Louis was terrified but he kept his eyes closed, trusting Akbar's wise words. Twenty seconds later... it was all over.

Louis opened his eyes as Barq slowed down and stopped.

He had won!

'*Well, I was wrong about this boy...*

'*He's certainly got what it takes.*'

TEN

Baby Turtle Stew

Next day, in the afternoon, Tizzie was one of the children scrubbing the deck when Squint shouted from the crow's nest.

'Giant turtles on the bow! A big bunch of 'em.'

'Whalemaster! More speed!' screamed Pigleg.

Thrackkkk!

The long whalewhip cracked with its distinctive sound.

Tugger and Trailblazer pulled harder.

Thrackkkk! Thrackkkk!

Tugger and Trailblazer pulled harder still.

The Revenger lurched into 'chase speed'.

The ship soon caught up with, and came alongside, the giant turtles. While all the pirates were looking at the water, Tizzie raised herself on her knees, in order to peer through the rails over the side of the ship.

The twenty or so turtles were huge. The largest was wider than the ship. There were four babies, but even the youngest was as big as an elephant.

One of the baby turtles craned its long neck to look up at the ship. It had big round eyes and a silly look on its face.

Oh it's soooh cute, thought the young girl.

'Who's for turtle stew, mates?' bellowed Captain Pigleg.

'I am,' shouted all the pirates in unison.

'Well make sure you take a littl'un,' ordered the Captain. 'We'll never haul a big'un aboard in one piece.'

With that, two rowing boats were lowered, each with a crew of seven. Six men rowed, whilst one stood at the bow armed with a sharp harpoon.

Tizzie couldn't bear to watch as the cute baby turtle was caught and towed back to the ship. She turned away and tried not to think about it as she busied herself with finishing her deck-scrubbing duties.

That evening, the hungry children were in the hold waiting for their rations. Normally they had stale bread or mouldy biscuits, and perhaps a little smelly cheese.

However, tonight, there was something different on the menu. They found this out when a big steaming pot was lowered down on ropes.

Mr Purgy followed the pot, huffing and puffing as he came down the ladder with a large ladle and lots of small bowls.

'We've got a real treat for you tonight, children. A real treat.'

'It's started already,' said Braz, a teenager from Lagutrop. 'We'll get proper food from now on. They're fattening the bait for the hunt. Making us tastier for Grunter.'

'Sshhh!' admonished Jack, nodding in the direction of the younger children, who would be terrified by his comment.

Tizzie looked up as Purgy ladled the scalding hot broth from the pot into the first of the bowls, describing it with relish as he did so.

'Baby turtle stew...

'Lovely.'

ELEVEN

Boiled Sheep's Eyes

Louis looked back down the race track.

They had run a *very* long way in a *very* short time.

After riding at a much slower pace back to the tents, Louis was first congratulated by Hans.

'Vell done, Louis. Vhen you let go of ze reins, I expected you to fall off.'

Louis beamed as he dismounted. He was, he had to admit, rather pleased with his effort.

'I nearly did fall off but I remembered what Akbar said and held on tightly to the saddle with my legs.'

As Louis and Hans walked to meet Akbar, they could see he was deep in whispered conversation with the same men as before. The sheik finished his discussion and came towards them.

'First things first, well done little warrior.'

Louis beamed again.

'As agreed earlier,' continued Akbar, 'they have sent a messenger bird to the Saalung lady who can help us in Nwotegroeg. Her name is Joyous Jilla.'

'But she's a Saalung!' exclaimed Hans. 'Zey're on Evile's side. Can she be trusted? Ve don't vant to valk into a trap.'

'I understand your concern,' answered Akbar. 'But not all the Saalung support Evile's Empire. Some of them are good people. Like Joyous. She runs the inn in Nwotegroeg but, secretly, she is also the leader of the rebels in that area. A very long time ago,

Clevercloggs the Explorer saved her great-great-great-grandmother from a fate worse than death at the hands of the Emperor.'

Both Hans and Louis opened their eyes wide with curiosity. Akbar could see they were itching to know more.

'But, that's a long story. A tale for another time. For the moment, it will suffice to confirm to you that it is for very good reason that the Jilla family has been totally loyal to Clevercloggs and the rebel cause ever since those events long ago.

'Joyous will take action when she receives the message that we are on our way to save Princess Tizzie. I am sure she will do whatever she can to help. I have asked her to send some men to meet us at the river with boats. If they are her men, they will know the passphrase. But for now, we must rest. And feast.'

With that, they walked a short distance and entered the Feasting Tent.

All the Blue Turbans were sitting on carpets and cushions on the ground.

There was great interest taken in Louis, the boy prince from Eporue who could ride like the wind.

'Here, a winner's seat,' said one of their hosts.

Louis now knew he had made the right decision when choosing to race. These people respected bravery and they were more likely to go out of their way to help someone who displayed it. He was prepared to do everything possible to rescue Tizzie, including risking his own life to make an impression on those who might be able to help.

Louis sat down and the man next to him held out a plate with small round things on it. The young boy was in such a good mood he took one without question.

'Ah, my favourite,' said Akbar, as Louis put the round thing in his mouth.

Snfff!

Hans didn't like the smell of the food. He turned up his nose. 'Vot are zeese?'

'Boiled sheep's eyes,' said Akbar, just *after* Louis had closed his teeth and burst the contents of the rubbery ball of food onto his tongue.

Squlch.

A gooey liquid oozed around his mouth and slithered down the back of his throat.

He felt sick.

But he *had* to swallow.

It would surely be very rude to spit it out.

Since he'd eaten the first one, the same man held out the plate of boiled eyes in front of him again.

Louis didn't know how to say '*no*' without offending his hosts.

He picked up another eye and put it in his mouth.

Squlch.

This was going to be a long night.

TWELVE

The Wassu Stone Circle

Unlike Louis, Clevercloggs had said the correct words when entering Godolphin's Crystal Door: 'Nwotegroeg, Aibmag, Jungleland, Acirfa'.

So it was that the intrepid little gnome, along with the other members of the rescue team – Princess Kea, Mr Sand, and Misty, the little blue mouse – were transported there by the ancient magic of Godolphin the Great.

They appeared, just as intended, inside a circle of redstones called the Wassu Stone Circle. This was a place of ancient magic, situated near the village of Ussaw, just south of the town of Ruatnuk.

Misty was still in the gnome's pocket. He didn't know anything about Jungleland and, being ever eager to learn, asked Clevercloggs a thought question.

'*Why didn't we just arrive in Nwotegroeg?*'

'Because Godolphin, a powerful and wise magician, would only use suitable and safe places for his transportation system. The Wassu Stone Circle is quite simply the nearest suitable and safe ancient magical gateway for us to arrive at when using the Crystal Door.'

Clevercloggs then proceeded to remove his extendable walking sticks from his belt so that he could get around better.

If you had to choose three people to rescue you from a difficult predicament, your initial choice, on first appearances, may not be the three who had just arrived in Jungleland.

In fact, it almost certainly would not be these three; a very slight teenage girl, a rather portly old man... and a tiny quincentenarian gnome with bad legs.

But you would be very wrong if you thought that way.

Tizzie and Louis could not have hoped for a better qualified and more heroic group of rescuers than those who had arrived to help them.

Kea of Kernowland was a fearless warrior princess.

Although still young, only just sixteen, she had, from a very early age, been brought up as the warrior-daughter of the ruler of a brave and good little kingdom, which unavoidably found itself in a continuing war with an oppressive evil empire. She was therefore a well-trained fighter who could think and act decisively in a scrap. On top of that she was an accomplished athlete, swimmer, and gymnast.

Gwithian Sand, wurld surveyor and mapmaker without equal, had a vast knowledge of Erthwurld and all its lands.

Although a very modest man from whom you would never hear it, he also had an enviable background as a colonel in the Kernish Army Special Forces. With seven decorations for gallantry and service beyond the call of duty during operations and skirmishes in the never-ending battle with the Empire, he had also been the only soldier in the history of Kernowland to receive the Kernow Cross – the kingdom's highest award for bravery – no less than *three* times in his thirty-year military career.

Clevercloggs the Explorer was, quite simply, a *living legend*.

At just under two-and-a-half feet tall, he was a somewhat diminutive hero, even for a gnome. Yet he had become a renowned martial arts expert and weapons specialist, having studied every form of offence and defence on all the eight continents of

Erthwurld. An acknowledged genius and polymath, amongst his many talents he was an accomplished scientist, mathematician, inventor, philosopher, artist, and musician.

But his greatest asset was undoubtedly his *experience* – he also had *five hundred years* of explorations, expeditions, exploits, and adventures behind him. Not only that, he was probably the best connected individual in Erthwurld. Many people, or members of their family, whether living or deceased, owed him a debt of gratitude for kind services rendered and freely given.

Of course the centuries had inevitably taken their toll, and the legendary gnome was a lot slower than he used to be; especially after the injuries to his legs sustained during a cowardly attack by the triple trolls of Tundraland.

But, even at this late stage in his long life, no one could deny that to have Clevercloggs on your side was still an advantage beyond measure.

And, if called upon, Misty could help too. He was a blue mouse, which meant that he had magical healing powers should anyone get injured.

All three rescuers were well trained in survival techniques.

On arrival at the stone circle, their first priority was drinking water. Princess Kea volunteered to find some and had soon located a small freshwater pool. Then, near the pool, they made a camouflaged jungle camp from bamboo and leaves, with a series of defensive traps and warning systems around it. It was in the trees, high off the ground, as a precaution against all the carnivorous jungle creatures they knew were in the vicinity.

This would be their operational base. From here they could plan and execute a rescue of Tizzie and Louis if and when the children arrived in Jungleland.

Kea and Sand listened to Clevercloggs as he stated his assessment of their position and priorities.

'Correct me if you disagree with anything, or have something to add…

'If we're going to have a chance of rescuing Tizzie and Louis, we'll need to gather local intelligence, to find out if, when, and where they'll be arriving.

'And we can only hope that Jack Truro, the Red Wizard's Apprentice, was indeed kidnapped by Pigleg and is still on *The Revenger* with Tizzie. Now that we know Evile has discovered *Skotos* the Death Stone – and has a Dark Magician evil enough to activate the Dark Beam – we must find that young man, wherever he is in Erthwurld. After the fall of the other Rainbow Wizards, he is the only person left alive in the wurld who may be able to wield Godolphin's *Amulet of Hope* and activate *Photos*, the *Crystal of Light*.

'But our little band is far too conspicuous to move around freely in Jungleland without being noticed. And since Manaccan has made us outlaws, enemies of the Empire, he'll almost certainly have put big rewards on our heads, so there'll very likely be bounty hunters, as well as the Empire soldiers, looking for us. Therefore, I suggest our next operational priority is to make covert contact with some members of RAE that I know in the area.'

'Right, good thinking, agree with all that,' said Princess Kea.

'Agreed,' said Mr Sand.

'They're the Jilla family,' continued Clevercloggs. 'The Jillas are based at the Jungleland Inn. It's an ideal "cover" and a great place for them to hear all the gossip about Jungleland and Erthwurld.

'The post office is just next door too. Which means the

messenger birds from around Erthwurld arrive only a few paces away from their front door.

'So, it goes without saying that the Jillas will be able to help with intelligence. The head of the family is Grandma Joyous.

'She's a real character.'

* * *

Clevercloggs made his way to the Jungleland Inn.

It was midnight. A party was still in full swing and music was blaring out of the wide-open windows and constantly swinging saloon doors.

The little gnome knew he couldn't afford to be spotted. He was, after all, a living legend in Erthwurld, and someone could easily recognise him.

He stayed in the trees as he made his way around to the back of the inn.

There was a pot plant in the garden, near the fence, with lots of small pebbles in it. The little gnome removed some of the pebbles and put a parchment note into the pot. Its contents would bring the Jillas up to date with his intelligence and plans, and request their own intelligence and help for the rescue of Tizzie, Louis, and Jack.

Then he carefully and quietly replaced the stones, which now completely covered and concealed the note.

His mission completed, the little gnome stole away into the jungle night.

THIRTEEN

Grunter's Weakness

The Revenger sailed on.

Tizzie was starving. She had had a very bad tummy ache all night from not eating anything in the evening.

The only breakfast on offer had been left-over turtle stew. Once again, the sensitive little girl just hadn't been able to bring herself to eat the baby turtle.

It was now lunchtime. Turtle stew… again. Tizzie was feeling very weak. The pain in her tummy was much worse and she began to contemplate actually eating the stew. But again she resisted.

After lunch, everyone heard Squint shouting very loudly from the crow's nest.

'Cap'n! Cape Edrev! On the port bow!'

'Anybody know anything about it?' asked Jack.

Braz told all he knew.

'Cape Edrev is a triangular-shaped piece of land that projects into the sea from the country of Lagenes. It's the westernmost point on the continent of Acirfa, a landmark for all sailors.'

'Oh yes, I remember that now from school,' said Anpaytoo. 'Sighting the cape tells sailors it's not far to Jungleland.'

'That's right,' said Braz. 'It means we should be there before nightfall.'

Up on deck, Captain Pigleg became agitated by the sighting of Cape Edrev. A look of hatred came over his face.

'Not long now, mates. We'll soon be there. And there's going to be one sorry pig in Jungleland when I catch up with 'im. But, fer now, I'm going to catch up with today's news. Purgy, get in my cabin. I need to talk to the tattoo.'

The tattooed pirate did as his captain asked but, as usual, he wasn't looking forward one little bit to what was going to happen next. Once in the cabin, Purgy slowly opened his tunic.

'Snnrrrr... Snnrrrr... Snrrrrr...'

Big Bessie was asleep, snoring soundly at two-second intervals on her bunk.

'Get on with it then,' chivvied his captain, glancing at Bessie as if he was slightly embarrassed about the noise she was making.

Luckily for Purgy, Tattow was, for once, easy to wake up. A light tap on his nose with his finger was all it took.

'Urghhh,' yawned the talking tattoo as he opened his eyes and saw Pigleg staring at him.

'Wassup Cap'n?'

'You know *wassup*!' scowled Pigleg, hardly able to disguise his irritation with this talking skin-picture that didn't show him anywhere near enough respect.

'Just tell me what's happenin' with The Big Pig.'

Tattow closed his eyes for a few moments.

'Oooo. Interesting. Very…' said the tattoo, tantalizingly.

'Well, what's the *news*?'

'My brother has word of a new development. Grunter has acquired a taste for the groundnuts they've been growing in Jungleland. He's been stealing them from the plantation fields.'

'Groundnuts?' queried Pigleg.

'Yes, Cap'n. They're called all sorts of names – earthnuts, goobers, goober peas, pinders, jack nuts, or manila nuts. And when they're in their pods, lots of people call them monkey nuts…

'But most people call them peanuts.'

'Ahhh, *peanuts*,' nodded Pigleg, leaning forward with interest as Tattow continued.

'Oooo. And there's more… Last night, the big red boar even raided the barns and ate five whole sacks of peanuts that had been shelled and salted ready for loading on the ships at Ruatnuk. Crashed right through the barn doors to get at them too. Seems to have developed a taste for the salted ones.'

'Sohhhhh, what's of particular interest about all that then?' queried Pigleg, a little dismissively.

'Well, Cap'n, my brother is suggesting that the boar's liking for salted peanuts may be his undoing.

'If he has an uncontrollable craving, perhaps that's a weakness which can be used to your advantage.'

Pigleg leaned further forward, his interest growing by the moment as Tattow continued.

'On previous hunts it has been hard to know where to look for him and most of the time has been spent searching in places where he was sighted or heard the day before. But he's always long gone by then.'

'That's true enough,' agreed Pigleg. 'He's one hard pig ta find, that's fer sure.'

'But what if you could bring the boar to you, Cap'n? What if you could lay a peanut trail and set a trap with the children *and* peanuts as bait? Surely the boar wouldn't be able resist the peanut trail and the double temptation at the end of it? If you set the trap well… Grunter would come to you!'

A look of understanding suddenly came over Pigleg's scarred and weather-beaten face. His eyes burned with hatred, and the hairs on his head smouldered like the embers of a fire.

FOURTEEN

The Animals Of Ainatiruam

Next morning, Louis and his companions left the camp of the Blue Turbans and set off into the desert.

The young boy was so happy that messenger birds had been sent and there was a good chance that friends would be waiting to help them in Jungleland.

He wasn't so happy to be desert-riding again.

After half a day spent swaying from side to side on the quadcamel and baking in the hot sun, Akbar suddenly spoke.

'We have entered the Sheikdom of Ainatiruam.'

Louis wondered how Akbar could tell. He looked around. To him, the desert still looked exactly the same in all directions. But he didn't ask any questions. He was conserving his energy for the gruelling day of quadcamel riding ahead.

Then, slowly but surely as they trudged on through the day, Louis noticed that the landscape was changing. He saw a dry type of grass growing in the sandy soil. Small bushes began to appear.

Akbar spoke again.

'As you can see, the desert starts to transform here. We are now entering a region called, the *Lehas*. You will now see many more living things.'

Hans already knew some of the animals of Ainatiruam and, for a while, he pointed them out as they rode on.

'A group of gazellelopes!'

'A haresquirrel over there.'

'And look, warthogfoxes!'

'A foxjackal!'

'Gerbilrats!'

After a while, Hans had exhausted the list of animals he knew. Then Akbar spoke again with a warning.

'From here, we must be on constant guard. There are also giant carnivorous beasts in this land which attack from all sides without warning.

'From beneath us, watch out for sandfishlizards. They swim through the sand and are clever pack predators. When they attack, one of them jumps out to grab the legs of your camel to unseat you. Then, when you are on the ground, another grabs your foot and drags you under the surface, where the pack devours you in seconds. Your only chance is to fire at the one that grabs your foot. That may cause the others to retreat. But you have to be ready… and quick.

'On the surface, cheetahleopard attack is the biggest danger. They are incredibly swift so you only get one shot before they are upon you.'

Louis was left wondering how anyone survived beyond childhood in this land, as Akbar continued.

'And lioneagles attack from the air. They swoop and take you from your saddle with their talons. You'll be taken off to a nest and fed to their cublets. It has happened to my good friends. All experienced warriors. So keep your weapons loaded and be ready to fire.'

The youth and the boy didn't need telling twice.

Hans checked his pistol.

Louis took out his catapult.

FIFTEEN

Smouldering Anger

As Pigleg's head glowed, tiny puffs of red smoke rose into the air above him.

This spontaneous combustion of his hair was a bodily function over which he had no control. When it happened, it reminded him of his terrible childhood and his thoughts now returned to that time. His mother was very poor and had accepted money to take part in a dubious mutationeering experiment when she was expecting him.

After her son was born, she had hidden the secret of his glowing red hair from everyone for as long as she could.

But, as he grew older, the boy became angrier and angrier, not least because his stepfather would beat him with a belt twice daily, just in case he had done anything wrong.

One day, having been beaten twice again for no good reason, the young boy got so angry that, lying on his bed in his room, seething at life's injustices, all the hair on his head ignited spontaneously.

The rag and straw pillow caught fire. And, in no time at all, the whole house burned down.

His stepfather thought he had started the fire on purpose.

After a severe belting, the young boy was sold to a pirate captain's wife, who had no children of her own. And the young boy had never seen his real mother again.

These, then, were just a few of the horrible childhood

experiences that would shape the warped and twisted personality of the most fearsome pirate in the history of Erthwurld.

Pigleg brushed away a rare tear with his hook as he thought back to that terrible time when he was taken from his mother.

'Are you all right, Cap'n?' asked Purgy, with genuine concern for his master.

'Yes, yes,' answered Pigleg, annoyed with himself that he'd shown weakness in front of one of his men. 'Be off with ye, man. Get back to yer duties.'

'Aye, aye, Cap'n,' said Purgy, as he turned and left the room.

Snnrrrr... Snnrrrr... Snrrrrr...

Now engrossed in his thoughts and oblivious to Bessie's snores, Captain Pigleg's mood brightened considerably as he thought about how he was going to use Grunter's craving for peanuts against him. And so finally exact retribution on the big pig that took his leg.

'I *will* have my *revenge*!' he growled, thumping his fist on the table as he jumped up from his seat and hurried to the door to shout after his tattooed crewman.

Click, thud. Click, thud. Click, thud.

'Purgy!'

'Yes, Cap'n?'

'Bring me rum and me cheeseboard...

'I need to plan.'

SIXTEEN

Gumbrella Trees

Louis and his companions travelled on through the land of Ainatiruam, constantly on the alert in case of carnivore attack.

Eventually, the dry grassland became dotted with strangely shaped trees, which had thorny branches and dark green leaves.

Louis voiced his thoughts.

'They look a bit like umbrellas.'

'Interesting that you should say that,' said Akbar. 'They're acacia trees. They can grow in areas such as this, with very low rainfall. Very useful too.

'For a start they produce a gum, which is drained from cuts in the bark. The gum is used in food and sweets – things like chewing gum, gumdrops, and marshmallows. It's also used in crafts and cosmetics. It has medicinal uses too; for lots of problems, like inflamed skin and fevers. The gum is used as a glue and as a binder in ink and paint. And for boot polish. And even in fireworks.

'The wood of the tree is used for tool handles and things such as parts for weaving looms. Rope and cords are made from the roots and bark. The nuts are edible too. And giraffephants eat the leaves. As do quadcamels! Yes, all in all, a very useful tree.'

Louis thought it was amazing that one tree could have so many uses, and he nodded to show he was listening and interested as Akbar continued.

'And, as you say, they're shaped a bit like an umbrella. Very good for sheltering under. Put the gum together with umbrella, and you get what we call acacias: *gumbrella trees.*'

Later in the day, Hans spotted a herd of one of his favourite animals.

'Look, giraffephants.'

Louis looked. The giraffephants were a strange looking mutant. They had the body of an elephant but the long neck and head of a giraffe. There were no tusks. They also had the colouring and markings of a giraffe, although he thought maybe a bit greyer.

The giraffephants were eating from the gumbrella trees.

'They feed all day,' said Akbar, 'sometimes for twenty hours. They've got long black tongues which they can wrap around the leaves of the tree and pull each leaf off without getting hurt by the sharp thorns. And, just like camels, they don't need much to drink so they can go for days without water in this dry region.'

That night, they camped beneath the shelter of one of the gumbrella trees. Louis looked up into the branches of the acacia, trying to remember all the uses of this very special tree as he drifted off to sleep.

SEVENTEEN

The Jaws of Jungleland

The Revenger arrived at the mouth of the River Aibmag in the early evening.

'Whalemaster! Work those steeds!' bellowed Pigleg.

Thrackkkk!

The whalemaster did as instructed.

Thrackkkk!

The sound of the long whalewhip cracking punctuated their progress, and the pirate ship made good time as it headed for Port Lujnab. Mangrove swamp lay on both sides of the river estuary.

The swamp was a thick, impenetrable mass of trees, its edges drowning under grey-green water.

As the ship sailed between the two rows of sunken trees, a hush came over the men on board. Whatever they were doing, the pirates all stopped it at once, and stared in silence at the awesome sight ahead. The two bands of trees slanted towards each other into the distance, giving the impression that the men were sailing into a huge, gaping mouth.

'The jaws of Jungleland,' mumbled Pigleg to his first mate. 'This place will swallow a man whole if he's not constantly on his guard, Mr Cudgel. It's a land of a thousand dangers. Warn the men to be vigilant at all times.'

'Aye, aye, Cap'n,' replied Mr Cudgel in a sombre tone, as if he were being overly respectful at a funeral.

'I'll spread the word... But I'm sure they already know.'

EIGHTEEN

Zonkeys

Next day, Louis was becoming very weary as they journeyed further and further south.

In the late afternoon, he was glad to see a town on the horizon.

'Yaruog,' said Akbar. 'The last place in Ainatiruam. Once there, we can take the ferryraft across the river. Then we can get some supplies at the Lumo on the other side before travelling on to Jungleland.'

'What's the Lumo?' asked Louis.

'The weekly market,' replied Akbar. 'We'll have to stay in Yaruog overnight as the next ferryraft won't cross again until tomorrow morning.'

That night, they slept just outside the town, using their saddle bags as pillows.

In the morning, Louis' neck was very stiff from sleeping at an awkward angle. But he didn't complain as they got up and headed for the crossing point.

There was a trading post near the ferry house.

'We'll have to trade the quadcamels here,' said Akbar. 'They'll never let such large beasts on the raft. We'll get some zonkeys. They're strong pack animals, and very suited to the terrain on the other side.'

Louis was itching to ask what a zonkey was, but he daren't for fear of giving himself away.

He soon found out when Akbar had concluded the deal. They

were zebradonkeys – half zebra and half donkey – called 'zonkeys' for short.

Akbar got five zonkeys for the two quadcamels. He wasn't content.

'A bad bargain, they're worth at least six zonkeys each.'

However, as usual, he was quick to be pragmatic.

'But we can't take the quadcamels any further. And these pack animals are ideal for the terrain across the river. It is a hilly region called *Little Mountains*. And at least we've got one mount each plus two to carry what we'll need.'

Louis learned that his zonkey was called Faloo.

'*Glad I got the kid,*' said a voice in Louis' head as he led Faloo the short distance to the ferryraft. '*The other humans look heavy and I don't want to carry a pack. It's always such hard work in this heat.*'

'Glad I got this zonkey, he's great,' said Louis out loud, knowing that Faloo would hear him.

NINETEEN

Thundershot

Port Lujnab was a sleepy outpost of the Empire. Its white-walled houses had green shutters at the windows, and sloping red roofs. Tall trees rose around and between the houses. Evstika flags fluttered everywhere in the breeze.

The Revenger docked at the long wooden pier that jutted into the river.

'Mr Cudgel, I want supplies for our little expedition into the jungle. Get a shoppin' party organised. I'll be comin' along too. I want to make sure we get all the right stuff.'

'Aye, aye, Cap'n,' said Cudgel. 'Purgy, you heard the Cap'n. Shopping party required.'

Purgy gathered together some men.

Click, thud. Click, thud. Click, thud.

Pigleg accompanied them as they went down the gangplank.

Some of the slavechildren had to go along to carry.

Tizzie was one of them.

The first thing Tizzie noticed about Jungleland was the intensity and stickiness of the heat.

The second was the buzzing flies and biting insects.

The children were marched in a slave chain to the market. They were made to stand and roast in the sun whilst Pigleg spent and spent.

He bought strong nets, thick and thin ropes, long wooden posts, four big wooden boxes, and lots more.

'Jack, why is Captain Pigleg buying all this stuff?' asked Tizzie.

'He needs it for the Grunter hunt. This is his last chance to stock up. He won't be able to get everything he wants in Nwotegroeg.'

After his shopping spree at the market, Pigleg led them to a compound surrounded by a high, circular wooden fence, some way from the town. The fence curved away from them in both directions. Two huge wooden doorgates served as an entrance.

Tizzie wondered what was on the other side.

Pigleg rapped on one of the doorgates with his hook.

'Come on, Bango, come on,' he boomed.

One of the doors was pulled open, revealing an enormous junk and scrap metal yard inside.

A short, bald-headed Blackskin man now appeared around the doorgate to greet them, his brown leather apron covered in black grease and other stains.

'Ah, Mr Bango, very good to see you again,' said the Captain. 'We wish to purchase some supplies of a metallic nature.'

'*Certainly*, Captain Pigleg,' replied Mr Bango. 'You've *certainly* come to the right place for metal supplies.'

The man obviously knew he was going to do some good business this day. He could hardly disguise his glee, and rubbed his hands together furiously as he invited the pirates in.

'Take all the time you need, gentlemen. I'm *certainly* in no hurry to close today.'

With that, Pigleg issued his instructions.

'Mr Cudgel, if you please, I need plenty of ammo for me Thunder Gun. Enough thundershot to fill those four boxes.'

'Aye, aye, sir. Purgy, you heard the Cap'n. Get 'em siftin'.'

'Right, you lot,' said Purgy to the children, 'get searching around this yard for small bits of scrap metal. Nails, balls, anything… as long as it's no bigger than this… no bigger than this.'

As he spoke, the pudgy pirate held up a piece of metal about the size of a marble. 'And we need anything made of lead, no matter how big or small it is.'

Tizzie clambered all over the piles of old metal around the yard as she joined the other children in looking for the shot that she knew would later be used as ammo for Blunder Bess.

She also knew from what the other children had told her that any lead they found would be melted down into little shotballs.

After an hour or so of searching, Pigleg seemed satisfied.

'That should be enough to blast ten mutant boars off the face of Erthwurld,' he declared triumphantly, as he stared at the four big boxes of shot the young slaves had found.

'It *certainly* should be, Captain,' agreed Mr Bango.

Pigleg thanked Mr Bango and handed over a whole bag of gold evos.

'Please come again,' said Mr Bango, clutching the bag of coins with both hands. 'You are *certainly* welcome here any time, Captain.'

That *certainly* seems to be his favourite word, smiled Tizzie to herself, as she heard Mr Bango use it yet again. He puts it in nearly every sentence!

Some of the children were made to carry the four boxes full of shot.

The others were loaded up with all the other things the Captain had purchased.

Tizzie had two particularly heavy posts in her arms. She could barely lift them, and yet she knew she was going to have to carry them for half an hour on the way back to the ship.

But she also knew there would be big trouble, perhaps a lashing, if she failed in her task – or if she complained even a little bit.

Somehow, digging deep inside herself and using all her strength, she managed to get the posts back; finally stumbling along the dock, totally exhausted, in the early evening.

As the frail little girl boarded the ship and dropped the posts, she glanced behind to smile weakly at Jack, who, along with another boy, had been made to carry the heaviest box of shot for the Captain's thunder gun.

Jack managed a faint smile back as Pigleg boomed his orders.

'Right lads, let's stow this stuff and be underway…

'LOOK LIVELY THEN!'

It was clear that the Captain was a pirate in a hurry.

As she was waiting in line to go down into the hold with the other children, Tizzie could just make out what Pigleg said to Mr Cudgel.

'Next stop… slave island.'

TWENTY

Slave Island

Having left Port Lujnab loaded with Captain Pigleg's purchases, *The Revenger* sailed on up the river.

They were getting deeper and deeper into Jungleland and, with every hour that went by, Tizzie felt as if she was getting further and further away from Louis.

The river was still very wide, and the swamp of submerged trees still lined its banks.

They were heading for a small island in the middle of the river called 'Semaj Island'. But it was a place better known to all pirates – and indeed the whole of Erthwurld – under another name...

Slave Island.

Tizzie and the other children had been taking it in turns to climb up and look through a couple of small cracks in the hull of the ship, one on the port side and one on the starboard side.

It was Tizzie's turn again as they approached the island.

She gazed through the hole.

The most striking feature on the island was a very old building.

'Can you see the fort?' asked Yang excitedly.

'Yes,' said Tizzie.

'My turn next,' said Yang.

Tizzie studied the fort. It had dirty walls that had once, a very long time ago, been white, and huge iron gates with a rusted sign above them.

Trees surrounded the fort, which had been there so long that it looked as if it was growing out of the ground.

'Fort Semaj,' said Jack ruefully. 'Gold, ivory, and slaves are kept there before being shipped around the Empire. It's an infamous prison. The slaves are kept in terrible dungeons, full of dirt and disease. The whole place is full of bedbugs, fleas, lice, ticks, and mites.'

'And, as well as ordinary fleas,' added Yang, 'they say there are burrowing fleas that tunnel into your bottom while you're asleep.'

'And jumping cockroaches too,' said little Lucy.

Sounds horrible, thought Tizzie; how can people be so nasty to other people and keep them locked up in places like that?

But before she could say anything, she and the other children heard Captain Pigleg shouting up on deck.

'We'll be dropping anchor for the fort, Mr Cudgel.'

'Aye, aye, Cap'n,' came the reply.

There was lots of activity on deck as the ship prepared to stop near the island. The pirate leader went ashore in a rowing boat with Cudgel and Purgy. Another boat followed on behind, carrying four heavily-armed pirates.

'Why are we stopping at the fort, Cap'n, if I may be so bold?' asked Mr Cudgel on the way there.

'Grunter has shown a taste for the local childmeat. So I want some local bait. He might prefer it. Just coverin' all the angles.'

'Good thinking, Cap'n,' said Cudgel admiringly.

Waiting for them on the jetty were six soldiers.

'Empire troops, Cap'n,' whispered Mr Cudgel. 'Is this wise? What about the Empire Arrest Warrant and the price on your head? And mine, come to that. And Purgy's. And all…'

'Nothin' to fear for us here, Mr Cudgel,' interrupted Pigleg.

'I know somethin' about the commandant that he wouldn't want anyone else to know, if you get my meanin'. So, as I say, nothin' to fear here.'

The pirates were taken to see Colonel Suntukung, an officer in the Empire Army. On first appearances, he seemed like any other officer. But it was soon clear that he was a little unorthodox.

'We have over one hundred adult slaves here at the fort, Captain Pigleg. Many are fit young men, very suitable for hard labour. The official Empire price is twenty evos for a strong young buck. But that's negotiable if you're willing to make a contribution to our... er... *benevolent fund*?'

Pigleg shook his head.

'We just want the young'uns. Under thirteens... Grunter bait.'

'Oh, yes of course, Captain.'

'And I was thinking that, if I get a *very* good price, Colonel, I may not start my memoirs... just yet.'

'Ah. Right Captain. I've just remembered that there is a special deal on child slaves. For today only. How about one evo per child?'

'Done. How many have you got?'

'Eleven.'

'Mr Cudgel, pay the Colonel.'

'Aye Cap'n,' said Cudgel, very surprised at the speed and generosity of the deal.

The slavechildren were dragged from the dungeons in chains, marched down to the jetty and loaded into the rowing boat.

'Eleven slaves for eleven evos. What a bargain,' said the first mate as the pirates returned to *The Revenger* with their purchases.

'It's what you know about who you know that makes all the difference in this wurld, Mr Cudgel.'

'Aye, Cap'n. So it seems.'

TWENTY-ONE

The Banquet of Peace

One of the first proclamations by Manaccan the Merciless had been to declare a *State of Emergency* because the murderous Prince Louis of Forestland had blown up the Forcesphere and made way for the invasion. This allowed the new King to impose martial law and consolidate his control of the kingdom.

Another proclamation was to declare the need for a *Banquet of Peace* to appease the invaders and pave the way for negotiations with the Empire.

The eight invader warlords – who led the invasion from north, south, east, and west – had occupied the whole of Kernowland with their armies. These warlords were now on their way to Kernow Castle with their highest ranking officers and their entourages, each looking forward, not only to the banquet in their honour, but to claiming their victor's prize... the hand in marriage of the beautiful Princess Kea.

Mrs Portwrinkle had been given specific instructions to cater for all the different tastes of the guests.

It had been a hard job to decide on a menu and cook food for people from so many different lands. She had first consulted her huge library of cookbooks from all over Erthwurld. Then she had gathered together all the ingredients. Finally, she had worked flat out with her kitchen staff, cooking almost non-stop for two days.

The result was a sumptuous spread of all different types of food, lined up on long tables in the Banquet Hall.

Pemberley had worked equally hard making sure everything else was ready. He and Mrs Portwrinkle had decided that it would be a good opportunity to gather information for RAE if lots of Empire generals and their officers were coming to the castle.

So they had no reservations about making it appear as if they were trying their best to make the banquet a success.

The warlords were introduced by Pemberley as they arrived and entered the great dining hall.

The loyal butler was, underneath his cool exterior, seething with anger that these enemies of Kernowland were being received as honoured guests.

He knew, of course, that he had to play his part well if he was to gather intelligence. But that didn't make it any easier, and some of the names nearly got stuck in his throat as he announced them.

'Hrappr Bloodaxe, Warlord of the Vikings.'

'Murdo McStabber, Warlord of the Highland Tocs.'

'Shawn O'Shorne, Warlord of the Eriemen.'

'Ali Blabla, Warlord of the Moors.'

'Gerard de Gall, Warlord of the Gauls.'

'El Toro de Torremolinos, Warlord of the Guerreros.'

'Angar Saxxon, Warlord of the Angles.'

'Shaka Shakabantu, Warlord of the Zulus.'

TWENTY-TWO

Two Tribes

The children who had just been brought aboard at Slave Island sat together at one end of the hold. They were itching and scratching, suffering terribly from the awful conditions of the fort dungeons.

Luckily, Janxa, one of the older girls, had grabbed some plants as she was being marched back to the ship.

With Masai's help – and the water rations of all the other children – she had made a natural lotion to soothe the bites and sores of the fort children.

Once the fort slaves were more comfortable, Jack spoke.

'Janxa, we want to learn everything we can about Jungleland. The more we know, the more likely we are to be able to survive if we escape. Can you tell us some things we need to know?'

'I'll try,' replied the twelve-year-old.

'At the mouth of the river, there are two swamps, the North Swamp and the South Swamp. Further up the river, the land rises and the jungle gradually becomes denser and denser. A long way up river, there is a steep rock face and a huge waterfall.

'The northern bank is the home of the *Saalung*. They are the majority, dominant tribe. They support the Empire and follow Evile. The *Bulubaa* tribe, my people, are south of the river. We live in constant fear of the Saalung, who cross the river all the time... on slaving raids. Most of the slaves are needed for the peanut plantations. But some of the stolen Bulubaa people are sold to Evile's slavemasters at Fort Semaj. It's horrible. We're kept in the dungeons until being taken away on ships to work as slaves around the Empire. That's what happened to me. They grabbed me while I was collecting plants near the riverbank. I need them for medicine for my mother; she's very sick.'

Tizzie thought it must be terrible to live in constant fear of being captured and sold into slavery.

'My tribe are a proud people,' continued Janxa. 'We fight back as best we can. We struggle against the Empire's slavery system and are fiercely loyal to the rebel cause. But we are outnumbered five to one, and the Saalung have the backing of the Empire forces, so it's very hard to keep up the resistance.'

After the lesson, Tizzie and the other children took it in turns to look through the cracks in the hull of the ship.

She saw all sorts of strange plants, animals, birds, and insects.

One of the children knew the names of all the birds. 'Look, there are pink-backed pelicans, and reef herons, and black kites.'

There was a very weird fish that kept jumping into the air and splashing back down in the water.

'Flying barracudas,' shouted Yang, excited, as ever, by any sort of mutant.

'And hump-backed dolphins,' shouted Meda. 'They're my favourite animals. I love to watch them jumping out of the water and splashing down when they play.'

It was then that Tizzie spotted a particularly strange animal in the trees that looked like it was a cross between a bird and a monkey.

The curious young girl was itching to ask what it was but didn't want to give herself away in case she should know.

Then she saw there were lots more of them.

They were gathering into a group and chattering furiously.

It looked like they were actually *talking* to each other!

TWENTY-THREE

Evile's Edicts

Manaccan the Merciless was very satisfied with the way the Banquet of Peace was progressing.

As he surveyed the gathering from his chairthrone at the banquet table, the teenage King was reflecting on his recent good fortune.

Whilst scheming for Darkness Day, he had promised *all* of the visiting warlords the hand in marriage of Princess Kea, as a reward if they helped with the invasion. But, at the time, he'd had no idea how he was going to keep to the promise since only one of them could actually marry her.

Then, in an amazing stroke of luck, his cousin had stabbed him and run away with Sand and Clevercloggs, meaning that *none* of them could have her.

So, it was 'problem solved'… for the time being at least.

Interestingly, given they had shown so much interest in the idea in the first place, none of the visiting warlords seemed particularly disappointed that Princess Kea had turned out to be a traitor and was now an outlaw on the run. They were apparently quite happy being entertained by the other ladies at the banquet.

Manaccan now decided it was time.

He clapped his hands and everyone stopped what they were doing immediately and looked towards the chairthrone.

Mr Lister entered the room and walked towards the head table, muttering one of his favourite lists as he went.

The Counterupper halted when he was behind and slightly to the left of King Manaccan's seat.

Unravelling the very wide and long roll of parchment he was carrying, he began reading very slowly, as if he was relishing every single lovely letter of his newest list.

'These are the Ten Edicts of the Emperor. They are *Imperial Law* throughout this new dominion of the Empire with immediate effect...

Edict Number I

This territory is henceforth to be known as the new Empire Kingdom of 'Wonrekland'; and the Emperor's Slaving System is hereby instituted. As a punishment for the long-time resistance of this territory against the Empire, one child from every family will be sold into slavery. A 'child', in this instance, will be defined as any youngling aged 12 or under at today's date.

However, in his beneficence – and as proof of his kind, thoughtful, and considerate nature – the Emperor will allow the parents of multiple younglings to choose which one of their children is sold as a slave.

Edict Number II

All gnomes and other sub-human species to be enslaved with immediate effect.

Edict Number III

Wonrekland will be divided into eight Regions. The eight victorious Warlords will each be granted a region, in recognition of their services to the Emperor.

Edict Number IV

The Parliament of Bards is no longer required. The Victorious Warlords will run their territories according to Imperial Law, under the rule of the new King of Wonrekland: Manaccan the Merciless. It is, henceforth, a capital offence to speak or write the old name of this territory without the Emperor's permission.

Edict Number V

The Kernowland Crown coin is hereby replaced by the Empire Evo. Taxes will be collected by King Manaccan on behalf of the Emperor. One half of the earnings and profits of all free citizens will be paid to the King, who will remit one half of all monies collected to the Emperor, the balance to be used for the administration and defence of Wonrekland. All free citizens will be allowed to keep slaves to help them earn enough to pay the taxes.

Edict Number VI

In addition to the change of name of the Kingdom, the names of the main towns will also be reversed according to the system favoured throughout the rest of Erthwurld by the Emperor. With immediate effect, Truro will become Orurt, Camborne will become Enrobmac, Penzance will become Ecnaznep, and Bodmin will become Nimdob.

Edict Number VII

Empire Military Service for all citizens of fighting age begins today. All citizens are required to wear the Evstika armband when in uniform.

Edict Number VIII

The Emperor's emblems and effigies will be prominently displayed throughout Wonrekland, including an Evstika flag on every public building, a statue of the emperor in every town square, and a picture and bust in every house.

Edict Number IX

The Empire Educational Curriculum will be adopted in schools. All existing teachers will be replaced with those officially sanctioned by the Emperor.

Edict Number X

A new colosseum will be constructed with immediate effect from the existing stadium at Enrobmac. It will be known as the *Conquest Colosseum*, in recognition of the Emperor's victory over this territory. Each village and town is required to provide at least one gladiator per hundred people for the Conquest Colosseum. The Warlords in each Region will be responsible for ensuring that there are sufficient volunteers. The first *Emperor's Games* will be held on the forthcoming Victory Visit of his Imperiousness to Wonrekland.

Throughout the whole reading of the edicts, Manaccan the Merciless had a nasty smirk on his face, as if he was very pleased with himself.

He couldn't help thinking about all that *tax* he was going to get from everyone. Even if he had to give half of the money to the Emperor, there would still be *such* a lot left over.

After all, he had only recently turned eighteen, and just the thought of *all that gold* was making him *so* excited about his new job.

TWENTY-FOUR

Parroboons

Tizzie was still looking out from the hold, her gaze fixed on the strange bird-monkeys that were perching in the trees along the riverbank.

Luckily, Janxa spoke again, telling the younger children about them without Tizzie having to ask.

'If you look through the crack in the hull, you'll see the parroboons. You can't miss them. They're multi-coloured and have two legs with clawed feet and two monkey hands on the end of short hairy arms.'

'And they've got a strange beakmouth,' added Yang, 'with very sharp teeth inside it.'

'Yes, that's right,' agreed Janxa, as she continued with a warning. '*Beware* of these animals. They are sly creatures who work for the Saalung. Since the earliest mutationeering experiments, they have been able to talk. But they don't just mimic sounds in a cute way like parrots, they *understand* what they're saying.

'Of course, they're not that clever, so they only use a small vocabulary of words they have learned. Their favourite word is *chop*, which is the local word for *food* in Jungleland. It's the word they all learn first.

'The second word they learn is *jongo*, which means *slave*. They all know that they will get a chop-reward of banananuts if they help catch a jongo. That's why they're always spying on the

Bulubaa people, to see if they can help send one of them into slavery. So, however cute they seem, *never, ever* trust a parroboon. They've always got their food reward in mind and would sell their best friend for a bag of banananuts.'

Tizzie made a mental note to be wary of parroboons.

At that moment, Purgy interrupted the lesson by shouting into the hold.

'Right, all of you on deck now.'

Tizzie went on deck with the other children. To her surprise, she was immediately handed a bunch of banananuts.

Click, thud. Click, thud. Click, thud.

Pigleg hurried over to the port side of the ship and whistled a very shrill sound into the North Swamp.

'Over here, me luvvlies,' he shouted, like an excited little boy. 'Over here. Come 'n' get it.'

Within seconds, about two dozen parroboons flew out of the trees. They flapped their wings furiously as they crossed the water, as if they were racing to be first.

The strange creatures landed heavily on the port rail as they arrived.

'Jenny said she heard the men saying that Pigleg has a big soft-spot for parroboons,' informed Jack. 'Apparently he had one called, *Choppy*, for a pet, when he was a child. It was his best friend. He called it that name because it was eating all the time and he loved to feed it.'

'FEED 'EM, THEN!' bellowed Pigleg at the children.

Tizzie and her friends duly took their bunches of banananuts and began feeding the parroboons. She pulled a banananut from the bunch, put it between two fingers and tentatively held out her hand.

One of the bird-baboons sidled along the rail on its clawed feet, ruffling its wings and squawksaying a word as it did so.

'*Chop, chop... Chop, chop... Chop, chop.*'

Oh they're quite cute really, thought Tizzie, as she extended her arm further to offer the banananut.

'Here you are.'

The parroboon took the food gently in its beakmouth, gulped it down and squawksaid a word Tizzie didn't understand.

'*Abaraka.*'

'It means *thank you*,' said Janxa.

'They're not so bad,' said Tizzie. 'Look, this one's eating very nicel…'

Bite!

'Ouch!'

Suddenly, just as Tizzie was talking to Janxa, the parroboon lunged with bared teeth at the bunch of banananuts she was holding, biting three of her fingers in the process.

The startled girl dropped the food on the deck.

Blood poured from Tizzie's wound as the creature dropped to the deck, snatched up the food with its monkey hands and flew off the rail back towards the riverbank, squawkshouting triumphantly as it did so.

'*Chop, chop... Chop, chop... Chop, chop.*'

'Hahaha!' laughed Pigleg when he saw what the parroboon had done to Tizzie.

'Hahaha!' laughed the other pirates.

Tizzie put her other hand around her bleeding fingers to try to stem the blood.

Janxa and Jack came to her aid.

'Oh no you don't,' said Purgy as he pushed her friends away

from her. 'Get on with the feeding. Little Miss Troublemouth can look after herself.'

Tizzie had already discovered that this was a dangerous world where you had to learn to take care of yourself. Thinking quickly, she tore off a strip of her ragged clothes and wrapped it around her wound as a makeshift bandage.

That would at least stem the bleeding for now.

TWENTY-FIVE

Og The Ogreman

On the orders of the Emperor, Manaccan had saved the best until last at the Banquet of Peace.

Everyone around the Empire loved the Colosseum Games. There was a colosseum in every territory. The games were what kept the citizens happy. As long as they had their games to watch, they didn't care too much what the Emperor was doing – and that made them easier to rule over.

What was going to happen now was special. It had required the assistance of the Vikings and construction of a special tentraft, but everything had worked according to plan and Manaccan was very pleased that it had because it would make him look good.

The King clapped his hands three times, which was the signal for the Master of Ceremonies to speak.

Everyone listened as the MC read from his piece of parchment.

Following Edict Number X, regarding the construction of the Conquest Colosseum, His Majesticness, Manaccan the Merciless, is very pleased to announce the arrival in Wonrekland of the Emperor's Champion Gladiator...
    'OG... THEEEEE... OGREMAAAAAAAN!'

The MC said the name as if he was announcing a gladiatorial bout.
    'Yeeeeeeeeeeeeeeeesssss!'

72

'Og! Og! Og!

'Og! Og! Og!'

Pemberley was shocked by the riotous reaction of the warlords and their guests. They cheered and laughed and banged the tables.

The mild-mannered and sophisticated butler had never seen anything like it in the banquet hall.

Then the guests started chanting at the top of their voices, both the men *and* the women.

'We want Og! … We want Og! … We want Og!'

Then there was an eruption of noise as the Emperor's Champion entered the hall.

'Hooooorrrrrrrrrraaaaaaaaaaaaaaaaaaayyyyyyyyy!'

'Og! Og! Og!

'Og! Og! Og!'

The cheering and laughing and banging continued as Og strode down the hall towards the top table, where Manaccan sat enjoying the appreciation of his guests.

The ogreman held a half-eaten raw reindeer leg in one hand and his ironhammer – which rested on his shoulder – in the other.

Pemberley was aghast at the sheer size of the ogreman.

Like everyone else in Erthwurld, the butler had heard the tales of Og's prowess in the Colosseum of Emor, the Emperor's showpiece stadium in the capital of the Evil Empire.

Up until now, he had thought that these stories must surely be exaggerated. But, seeing Og in the flesh with his own eyes, he began to believe that the reports might be true. For a start, they said he was five paces long lying down. Well, standing up, he certainly looked at least that. They said he cracked open his opponents' heads, three or more at a time, with that ironhammer. That was now much easier to believe.

Pemberley had also heard some other things about the ogreman. He came from Fjordland, the home of the Vikings. He was made when a Fjordland mutationeer had mixed ogre and human cells. He fed on raw reindeer meat. Other than that, Pemberley knew very little. But he was certain that the arrival of this monstrous gladiator was not a good thing for his country.

Manaccan had decided to get the maximum kudos from having the ogreman at his first banquet. He stood up, waving his arm royally as he spoke.

'Warlords, honoured guests, I give you… Og.'

'Hooooorrrrrrrrrrraaaaaaaaaaaaaaaaayyyyyyyyy!'

'Og! Og! Og!

'Og! Og! Og!'

The cheering and banging began again.

Manaccan held up his hand to quell the enthusiasm.

'It gives me great pleasure to announce that the Emperor's Champion Gladiator is here to compete in the very first Wonrekland Games, which will begin at the Conquest Colosseum exactly one month from today.'

'Hooooorrrrrrrrrrraaaaaaaaaaaaaaaaayyyyyyyyy!'

'Og! Og! Og!

'Og! Og! Og!'

All the warlords and other guests cheered and laughed and banged the tables again as Og turned and strode back out of the banquet hall.

Pemberley was downcast.

He now realised just how bad things were going to be under the rule of Manaccan the Merciless and his master, Evile the Emperor.

How could his country and his people be saved from such evil and darkness?

TWENTY-SIX

Cule And Bella Go West

Cule Chegwidden had grown up on Darkness Day.

In a few short hours, he had been transformed from a fun-loving *youth* – enjoying surfsliding with his friends – into a *man*.

A warrior, fighting for his country.

He had saved lots of the old people in Towan Blystra from being eaten by the trogs.

They had thanked him by hiding him from the Empire soldiers as the conquerors entered Towan Blystra.

The soldiers made it very clear they wanted to find and execute whoever had killed the trogs, as the hairy monsters were one of the Emperor's favourite chewing creatures.

However, despite interrogating lots of people, they hadn't been able to persuade anyone to give Cule away. Everybody insisted they had seen nothing.

Knowing he couldn't fight so many battle-hardened soldiers on his own, and that it would make most sense to live to fight another day, the brave young warrior had quickly decided he had only one choice of action…

Escape to Acirema North.

This made a lot of sense. That land had been conquered by the Empire only a few years ago, well within living memory. The Redskins were a proud and good people. Cule knew there would be many amongst them who would remember what is was like to be free from the tyranny of the Empire.

And their leader, Chief Natahwop, although now quite old, was a legendary warrior and tactician. Perhaps he could be persuaded that the time was right to lead a wurldwide uprising against Evile, and help free Kernowland in the process.

After hiding for a few days in cellars and attics, the plans had been made to put Cule on a ship bound for Acirema North.

He was to be a merchant seaman, working his passage.

Cule was now aboard the ship as it sailed away from the land of his birth. He looked back at the rugged cliffs of his homeland with a tear in his eye.

It was then that he made a solemn vow, muttering the words under his breath and wiping away the tear as a look of steely determination came over his face.

'Whilst I still have breath in my body, I shall one day return… to drive this evil darkness from the land of Kernow.'

* * *

Unbeknownst to Cule, Bella Bodella was heading the same way as him.

Along with lots of other dolphineers on the north coast of Kernowland, she had found no invaders to fight during the invasion.

The sea forces of the Empire had all attacked the west and south coasts, leaving the airborne ramdragons to attack from the north.

On realising this, Bella and many other dolphineers had raced as fast as they could go towards Land's End. But sadly, by the time they got there, the invader had already landed.

It was then that the dolphineers had spotted the shattered remnants of the Kernish fleet.

The captains whose ships were still seaworthy had agreed that the best course of action was to gather as many of their fighting men and women as possible from the waters and beaches of their defeated kingdom and retreat in order to regroup to fight another day.

They had lost the *battle* but they knew they had Right and Good on their side... so they were convinced that, if they could keep on fighting, they would one day win the *war*.

The captains knew their best sanctuary would be Acirema North.

It was a big country, only recently brought under the yoke of the Empire, and there were plenty of places to hide and rebuild their forces.

Like Cule, they also hoped to contact Chief Natahwop and enlist the help of his countrymen to rid Erthwurld of Evile and his Evil Empire once and for all.

Thinking fondly of her family, friends – and Cule Chegwidden – Bella, and the other dolphineers, joined the battered and broken ships of the Kernish navy as it sailed.

And so it was that the surviving Guardians of Kernow – defeated but undaunted – headed west.

TWENTY-SEVEN

Monster Mosquitoes

'Tseeep!' 'Tseeep!' 'Tseeep!'

'Vvit!' 'Vvit!' 'Vvit!'

'Cheweeweewee!' 'Cheweeweewee!' 'Cheweeweewee!'

Next morning, a cacophony of birdsong greeted Tizzie as she awoke. There were chirrups and squawks and sounds she just couldn't describe in words.

'They call that the Jungleland Dawn Chorus,' said Jack. 'Means we'll be entering the real jungle soon.'

During the day, as *The Revenger* sailed on up the river into the Nawerek Straight, the river narrowed and the terrain changed.

The children looked out through the cracks in the hull and saw the swamps become denser jungle as the ship sailed deeper and deeper into Jungleland.

In the evening, as the light faded, all sorts of strange jungle noises could be heard from beyond the river banks.

What sort of animals make noises like that? thought Tizzie, hoping that she would never have to find out.

All the children had been issued with mosquito nets to sleep under. As Tizzie rigged her net up as best she could, she couldn't help thinking that it was pointless. Why bother with a net when the holes in it were so big that any mosquito she had ever seen could get through them easily?

Then she heard Jack explaining about Jungleland mosquitoes to the younger children.

'Make sure you set up your net properly. The jungle mosquitoes are mutant giants. Monsters. They can suck up a huge glug of blood in a second, and leave a sore lump the size of your fist that takes two weeks to go down.'

'And they spread airalam fever,' added Janxa. 'That's why Pigleg got us the nets. Grunter would smell the fever from far away. He wouldn't want to eat us if we get sick with it so we'd be useless as bait.

'It's a terrible illness. After the bite, you get the sweats and the shakes. And the chills. And a horrible headache, and other aches all over your body. And you'll get diarrhoea and be vomiting all the time as well. Thankfully, the fever kills most people in a few days so they don't suffer too long.'

With that truly terrible prospect in mind, Tizzie set her net for the coming night even more carefully.

Then she closed her eyes and tried to sleep, frightening herself still further by imagining all the dangerous creatures that might be making those noises on the riverbank.

Zzzzzzzzzzzzzzzz.

Just as she was getting off to sleep, the scared little girl was convinced she could hear a 'zuzzing' in the darkness.

Zzzzzzzzzzzzzzzz.

Was it a giant mosquito?

TWENTY-EIGHT

The Traitors Prosper

Like Manaccan, the other Darkness Day traitors had wasted no time in profiting from their treachery.

In particular, Lester Lister was doing very well. In fact, he was now earning twice his former salary.

But money wasn't that much of a concern to him.

It was his lists and the *power* and the feelings of importance they conferred that mattered to this otherwise insignificant little man.

On starting work for his new masters, the Counterupper had immediately set about revising the old lists of Kernowland into the new lists of Wonrekland.

His first visitor was Miss Wendron, the new *Regulator of Schools*.

'I'd like a list of all the teachers in the kingdom, so I can send them all a letter,' she said at their meeting. That was easy. Mr Lister already had the list from when he was doing the job of Counterupper for King Kernow.

Each of the teachers then received a very short letter. It had their name and address at the top and just two words on the page, written in capital letters...

YOU'RE FIRED!

Before she had even sent out the letters, the wrinkled old hag had already started interviewing new teachers from Angleland and other places around the empire. Since well before the invasion, she had decided she was going to get the nastiest teachers she could find. She hated Kernowkids and wanted to make them suffer as much as possible at school.

The next visitor to Mr Lister's office had been Sheviok Scurvy, the new *Chief of Police*.

'I need you to start a list of all people who might still be loyal to King Kernow and the old kingdom, and so be potential members of RAE. I'll have no rebels causing trouble on my watch. Especially with the Emperor due to visit soon.'

'Good idea, Mr Scurvy,' said Lister, very pleased that he was being asked to start a brand new list that would need memorising. 'What shall we call it?'

'*Rebels and Troublemakers*.'

'Oh, very goood,' said Mr Lister as he dipped his quill in the ink and put the heading at the top of a scroll of parchment. 'We'll do this alphabetically. Who shall we start with?'

'Addington, Joseph,' said Scurvy.

'What's he done?'

'He bullied me at school.'

'Very well, it's your list Mr Scurvy. Who's next?'

Scurvy paused as he tried to think alphabetically.

'Albaston, Florence.'

'And her crime?'

'Wouldn't marry me.'

'Who's next?' asked Lister, already enjoying this new list enormously… not least because it was going to be such a long one.

When he had helped Mr Lister create the list of potential rebels and troublemakers, Scurvy started a recruitment drive for the *Secret Police* – Evile's 'special security division' – the organisation which created such an atmosphere of fear and uncertainty amongst ordinary people throughout the rest of the empire.

At the same time, citizens of the newly-named Wonrekland were being encouraged to spy on their neighbours and report any anti-Empire thoughts or activity. Even children were told they would receive substantial rewards for telling on their parents.

But Scurvy had a hard time recruiting for his secret police. In fact, nobody at all turned up for the interviews. And nobody came forward to tell on their friends or family. It seemed that it would take more than a change of name and leadership to change how the people felt in their hearts.

So Scurvy and King Manaccan decided to bring in recruits for the secret police from outside. They arrived within days. One thousand of them. All men and women of dubious character who couldn't get jobs elsewhere.

Scurvy knew that, as an act of defiance, the good and loyal citizens continued to use 'Kernowland', the old name for their kingdom, in private conversation. And he also knew that they had made up a name for the newly-arrived secret police... *Scurvy's Scum*!

But he was prepared to let all that go for now, and bide his time on the basis that everyone would soon come into line when his new instrument of punishment arrived.

The *Guillotine of Sirap* was on its way.

Public executions would soon take place as a show of Empire power. That would create fear amongst those who may be leaning towards rebellion, and Scurvy was convinced that people would soon be showing him the respect he thought he deserved.

Manaccan joined Scurvy and Lister in working on the list of people who were to be executed. It now included:

Kea, Princess

Louis, Prince
Sand, Gwithian

Wendron had also made a suggestion for the list.

'You can stick the ex-teachers on there. They'll be cross they've lost their jobs and are likely to cause trouble. And they're no use anymore anyway, now that we've got Empire teachers arriving in the next few days. We're better off getting rid of them.'

'Very goood,' said Mr Lister, although it was more that he was pleased to be adding people to the list rather than that he agreed particularly with Wendron's reasoning.

Wendron started listing the names of the former teachers she could think of.

'Perfect, Petula.

'Prudent, Priscilla.'

'Oh no, Miss Wendron, it's quite all right,' said Lister, stopping her in mid-flow. 'I've already got the whole list of the teachers back at my office.'

'Very well,' said Wendron, 'but make sure you don't forget any of them.'

The wrinkled witch had also been very pleased to have received a Sky Safety Certificate for her Skycycles, and a drilling permit for Wendroileum. And she was delighted that permission to begin industrial scale production had been granted to her new company, *WENCO*.

The factory and drilling fields in Smog Valley would soon be churning out her flying machines and spewing out Wendroileum, and she had already decided on a name for the plant and its surrounding accommodation for workers...

Smogtown.

Wendron didn't want to pay workers. She knew it would be much cheaper in the long run to buy slaves. After the initial investment, there would be nothing more to pay except for a bit of gruel to keep them alive.

And, with the huge number of child slaves coming on to the market due to the Emperor's first edict, she would be able to negotiate a very good price for a bulk purchase.

Wendron couldn't wait. As soon as *Edict Number 1* was enforced, and one child from each family in Wonrekland had been delivered by Drym to *Maggitt & Maggitt*, the slave auctioneers, she was going to buy lots of them to work in her factory and drilling fields.

The Smogtown factory and fields were going to be open around the clock.

24 hours a day.

7 days a week.

365 days a year...

And *366* days in leap years.

TWENTY-NINE

They Eat You Alive

'Tseeep!' 'Tseeep!' 'Tseeep!'

'Vvit!' 'Vvit!' 'Vvit!'

'Cheweeweewee!' 'Cheweeweewee!' 'Cheweeweewee!'

In the morning, the Dawn Chorus greeted them once more. But now it seemed much louder.

'Clean that hold,' shouted Purgy, down through the hatch.

The unlucky ones, whose turn had come up on the rota, stayed behind whilst the others went up the steps.

Scrtch. Scrtch. Scrtch.

On deck, Tizzie scratched her head again. It had been itching all night. She looked around.

Scrtch. Scrtch. Scrtch.

All the other children seemed to have the same problem.

'I think some of the kids from the fort brought head lice aboard,' said Jack, as he scratched his head along with the others. 'Will your lotion work for it, Janxa?'

'No, I'm afraid not. We need something different for lice. I'll try to grab some of the tree bark for it when they take us off the ship.'

'Thanks,' said Jack.

Scrtch. Scrtch. Scrtch.

'Looks like we'll just have to scratch in the meantime.'

Tizzie wasn't sure she was supposed to hear what Janxa said next to Jack in a low voice: 'But no one has a cure for airalam fever. And little Lucy has been bitten. Shall we tell the pirates?'

Before Jack could answer, there was an excited shout.

'What are they?!' It was little Lucy, who was sitting on another girl's shoulders. She pointed towards the jungle before rubbing the big red sore lump on her arm.

Tizzie looked in the direction Lucy had pointed.

'Tree octopuses,' said Yang, who was a bit of an expert on all things mutant.

'They first crawled from the water after escaping from the early mutationeering experiments in this region. The mutationeers thought they'd try mixing monkey and octopus cells. The tree octopuses were the result.

'There are thousands of them now. They spend some time in the water to keep their bodies moist, and the rest of the time in the trees.

'They're carnivores...

'Pack hunters.

'Make sure you keep looking up above your head when you're in the jungle.

'They drop down on you and fold their armtentacles around your whole body so you can't move.

'And then they slowly eat you alive with their sharp beak.

'It's a horrible way to die.'

THIRTY

Burn-Blisters And Bottom-Burrowers

As *The Revenger* sailed on up the river, Janxa pointed out various landmarks.

'We're just passing the village of Abadnet,' she said, as she looked through the starboard crack. 'It's the halfway point between the coast and Nwotegroeg.'

Some time later, she spoke again.

'We've reached Oknok-Asnam. The river becomes much narrower here. And it changes colour because the sea water doesn't mix with the river water anymore. It's freshwater from now on.'

The terrain was changing again too. The riverbank rose on either side and the vegetation became yet more dense.

That night, there were even stranger jungle noises emanating from beyond the riverbank.

Was one of them Big Red Grunter?

Tizzie covered her ears and tried to think of her soft comfortable bed at home as she tried to get to sleep.

The following morning, she woke up with a sore left leg and a burning feeling in her right ankle. She thought at first that she had sunburn from being on deck. The sun was, after all, very strong in this region, and lots of the children had sore, peeling skin.

But the pain was a lot more localised and intense than ordinary sunburn.

At Jack's request, Janxa inspected Tizzie's leg.

There was a chain of blisters in a neat line near her knee and another chain around her ankle.

'They feel like burns,' said Tizzie. 'It's like someone has touched my skin with something round and very hot in lots of places.'

'Biting fleas,' said Janxa, matter-of-factly. 'They give you burn-blisters. As I said before, there are many different kinds of fleas, lice, ticks, and mites in Jungleland. Some live on you or in your clothing…'

'And others just visit to feed on your blood,' interrupted Yang, as if he would actually invite them on to his skin to bite him if he could.

Tizzie wanted to scratch her burn-blisters because they were itching so much, but Janxa had made it very clear she was not to, otherwise they might get infected and she could lose her leg.

She was feeling very sorry for herself until she saw that Janxa and Jack had moved on to attend to some of the other children who were suffering much more than she was.

They were the Bulubaa kids who had been in the dungeon at the fort.

Tizzie learned that six of them had been infested by the worst type of flesh-eating fleas known in Erthwurld…

Bottom-burrowers.

THIRTY-ONE

They're Watching Us

'We need to ask the Captain for permission to boil some water,' said Janxa. 'The children won't be able to sit down until they get rid of the bottom-burrowers. They burrow deep into the flesh of your bottom. The only way I know of getting rid of them is to squat over a bucket of boiling water and burn them out with steam.'

Jack asked Jenny if she would ask the pirates for boiling water. She agreed to try, then went to Pigleg's cabin and knocked on the door.

'Snnrrrr... Snnrrrr... Snrrrrr.'

She could hear Big Bessie's loud snoring from outside.

'Come in, come in.'

Jenny entered.

'Permission denied,' said the Captain, coldly, as soon as he heard the request. 'I remember I had a bad case of the bottom-burrowers when I was a lad. Nasty little things. Chewed and chomped away at me bottom-flesh day and night, night and day. Couldn't sit down for a month. But they eventually die off, dry up, and drop out when they've fed on you for a few weeks.'

'Oh, but Captain...'

'Sohhh...' interrupted Pigleg, 'we're *not* gonna be burnin' good wood to boil water to get rid of fleas that are gonna die anyway.

'Is that clear, girlie!?'

'Yes, Cap'n,' said Jenny, fearing that Pigleg may be beginning to lose his temper, because his hair was starting to glow.

Seeing no sense in asking again or arguing once the Captain had made his decision, she hastily retreated from the cabin.

'Snnrrrr... Snnrrrr... Snrrrrr.'

Jenny closed the cabin door to the sound of Bessie's snoring and made her way down into the hold to give everyone the Captain's answer.

Tizzie felt desperately sorry for the fort children when they were told the news. They were obviously very miserable and scared.

'Erherr.'

'Erherr.'

'Erherr.'

Even the older ones began sobbing uncontrollably.

'There, there, the biting will stop in a few weeks,' said Tizzie, as she cuddled one of the younger children who had been infested by the bottom-burrowers.

'*Erherr*!'

As soon as she said it, Tizzie realised that her comment would be of little comfort to a child whose bottom was actually going to be bitten incessantly for the next month or so.

Later that day, Janxa looked through one of the cracks in the hull in order to report where they were along the river. Dropping back down to the floor of the hold, she said to the others: 'It's the Uknuknad Bend.'

'What's that?'

'An "S" shaped curve in the river where it narrows and the forest gets much thicker. We're in the real jungle now.'

Up on deck, Pigleg issued a warning to his men.

'Watch out, lads.

'We've reached the dark Heart of Jungleland.

'The Bulubaa will want their children back.

'And you can be certain-sure of one thing…'

He paused as he pointed with his hook-arm held outstretched, slowly moving it in an arc.

'They're out there somewhere, in those trees…'

He paused again.

'Watching us…

'Waitin' fer their chance…

'To *attack*.'

THIRTY-TWO

Boarders On The Bow!

'Boarders on the bow!' bellowed Captain Pigleg.

Tizzie was in the hold with the other children.

She could hear the Captain barking out warnings and orders.

Then there was a huge commotion on deck.

The frightened young girl raced to climb and peer through a crack in the hull.

A flaming arrow flew from the trees on the riverbank.

It was heading straight for the ship.

Another arrow followed the first.

Then another.

'Put out those fires!' bellowed Pigleg.

Blackskin men in dug-out canoes were racing towards *The Revenger*.

Some were paddling with leaf-shaped oars.

Others were aiming darts from blow-pipes.

Two pirates fell into the water from the ship.

One had a flaming arrow in his chest.

The other a poison dart in his neck.

'Tell us what's happening, Tizzie,' shouted Jack.

Tizzie reported all she saw, as it happened.

'My people are coming for us,' said Janxa. 'They have waited for the narrowing of the river.'

The other Bulubaa children babbled excitedly in their own language.

Boom! Boom!

'They've got cannon!' bawled Pigleg.

Krshhhhhh!

Krshhhhhh!

Two cannonballs smashed through the hull of the ship, sending long sharp splinters of wood in all directions around the hold.

'Arghhhh!'

'Urghhhh!'

'Arghhhh!'

Some of the children cried out as they were hit by splinters.

There were no more cannon shots.

'They must have realised their shots missed the deck and hit the hold where we are,' shouted Janxa to Jack, as she did what she could to stem the blood dripping from a wounded, screaming child.

'What's happening now, Tizzie?' shouted Jack.

'The canoes have reached the ship.'

'And there are two rafts on this side, with lots of men on them,' added Anpaytoo, who was looking through another of the cracks. 'Janxa's people are throwing ropes with hooks and trying to get on the ship.'

'And they're throwing spears,' said Tizzie.

Four more pirates fell into the water as they were hit by the spears.

Pishh! Pishh! Pishh!

The pirates responded with pistol fire.

Bulubaa men fell from their canoes and rafts.

Then Tizzie heard another order from Pigleg above the battle noise.

'Prepare to repel boarders!

'Bring me me Thunder Gun!'

Seconds later, there was an explosion of sound.

THUBOOOOOOOOOOMMMMMMMMMMMMMM!!!

It was like a thunderclap overhead.

Ten or more of the boarders fell into the water at the same time.

Drmmm. Drmmm. Drmmm.

A very loud drum sounded from the riverbank.

The Bulubaa immediately ceased their attack and retreated.

'Haaarggghhhhhhhhhhh!' roared Pigleg triumphantly as he raised the Thunder Gun into the air above his head.

'They don't fancy tanglin' with Blunder Bess, eh lads!'

'Nay, Cap'n!' replied the crew in unison.

When the Bulubaa children heard what had happened, the younger ones started crying.

'Erherr.'

'Erherr.'

'Erherr.'

Tizzie and the others comforted them as best they could.

A heavy blanket of despair fell upon all the children in the hold.

THIRTY-THREE

The Peanut Port

The next day, *The Revenger* docked at a large jetty.

'Ruatnuk,' said Janxa. 'This is where the peanut plantations are. They call it the "peanut port".'

'Why do you think we're stopping here?' asked Jack.

'Not sure. I'd have thought Pigleg would want to get to Nwotegroeg as soon as possible.'

The children were all brought on deck.

'Right,' said Purgy, 'we're taking you ashore to the peanut factory. For carrying duties.'

'Piggyleggy!'

Big Bessie had emerged from her quarters and was staggering along the deck with a bottle of rum in her hand.

'Not now my pumpkin dumplin', said Pigleg, with a somewhat strained look on his face. 'I'm workin'.' He then tried to gently push his girlfriend back into the cabin from whence she came. 'Now, in you go. You did agree to stay in there until we get to your grandma's place.'

'Oh but I'm bored in that little room all the time,' said Bessie, very loudly. 'I need some *air*!'

Pigleg was just about to insist again when Bessie noticed the children lined up at the other end of the ship.

'Oohh look, sweet little kidlings. I'd like ten of them when we're married.'

Pigleg rolled his eyes upwards to show his disapproval of that idea as she barged past him and on along the deck towards the children.

'This is our chance. Look sick, and scratch all over,' whispered Janxa to Tizzie, 'and pass it on.'

Tizzie did as requested and the message went down the line. Scrtch. Scrtch. Scrtch.

All the children were itching and scratching even more frantically than usual as Big Bessie approached.

'Oh, poor little things,' said the big-hearted woman, with genuine concern in her voice. 'What's the matter with your heads and bottoms? And your skin looks so sore all over.'

'We've got head lice, burn-blisters, and sore bottoms from flesh-eating burrowing fleas,' said Janxa, trying to sound as sickly and forlorn as possible. 'We need medicine… I know how to make it from the jungle plants. And we only need some boiling water to get rid of the fleas.'

'Right,' said Bessie, as – with a very determined look on her face – she swivelled her massive frame on the heels of her high-laced boots and rolled back down the deck.

She spoke without looking at her boyfriend as she passed him by.

'*Piggy*. Can I have a *word*.'

'Well, as I said, I'm workin' at the…'

'*NOW*!'

'Okay, pumpkin,' said Pigleg, a little timidly. 'I suppose I can spare a minute or two.'

Pigleg followed Bessie into his cabin.

Moments later, Purgy was summoned there.

He emerged after a further few moments, waddling towards the children, looking decidedly downcast.

'Right. It's your lucky day. The Captain has decided that you can all have medicine for your blisters and lice when we go ashore. And you can make a fire to boil water to steam out the bottom-fleas.'

This news made the children very happy.

Janxa smiled knowingly at Tizzie and Jack. It was obvious to all the children that the Bulubaa girl's quick thinking had worked. Big Bessie had put her large foot down on their behalf, and Captain Pigleg had given in.

They were all marched down the gangplank. Janxa was allowed to collect the plants and bark required to make the medicine, which was then administered to all those who needed it.

Jack and some of the other boys collected wood and made a fire under a big cauldron of water. Once the water had boiled, the cauldron was moved behind a big bush. Each child with fleas in his or her bottom then took it in turns to go behind the bush and squat over the steaming cauldron. Very soon, everyone was feeling much better.

'Right,' said Purgy as soon as he saw they were finished, 'now get moving and look sharpish. We've wasted enough time on doctoring for one day.'

The children were marched to what looked like a massive farm. They walked under a sign at the entrance: *Ruatnuk Peanut Plantation*. Once inside, they were greeted by the sad sight of hundreds of slaves working in the fields. But they had little time to look as Purgy was soon pointing and issuing orders.

'You lot, pick up those sacks of peanuts. And you little ones, you can carry those bags of salt. And that barrel needs to go on that cart.'

The barrel was huge.

'Do you know why we're doing this?' asked Tizzie as Jack helped her heave a big sack of peanuts onto her shoulders.

'No idea,' said Jack. 'But I bet we'll find out soon.'

To the children's surprise, when they got back to the ship, the sacks of peanuts were dumped down in the hold with them.

Purgy came down the steps and opened one of the sacks by slitting it down the middle with his knife.

He then tipped the nuts from the sack, making a big pile in the middle of the hold. Then he slit a second sack. Then a third. Again he poured the unshelled nuts out on the pile. Then he poured three bags of salt on the floor.

'Right, you're to shell and eat all these peanuts tonight, Cap'n's orders. And make sure you dip them in the salt before you eat them. No water rations until everything's gone.'

The children had no idea why they had to eat all the peanuts and salt. But they were all very thirsty in the heat and wanted to earn the water ration, so they did as they were told and started crunching through them.

At first everyone agreed the salty peanuts were lovely and it was great fun playing a game of throwing and catching them in their mouths.

But, after a while, even Tizzie, who loved peanuts, agreed with her friends that eating so many at once was no fun at all, especially with all that salt on them.

It made their mouths *really* dry. And there were *so* many to eat before they could have any water. It was not until just before bedtime that all the peanuts from the three sacks were gone.

Purgy came to check they had eaten the whole pile.

'Okay,' he said grudgingly to the water monitor, after satisfying himself that all the peanuts and salt had been eaten up.

'Let 'em have their water ration.

'Half a ladle each.'

THIRTY-FOUR

The Boar Eats Their Children

It was midday. Nwotegroeg had been sighted on the bow.

'Prepare for docking,' bawled Pigleg.

The children were brought from the hold and lined up on the deck, ready for disembarking.

Tizzie could see that the town was on a large island in the middle of the river. Looking ahead, Janxa spoke.

'That's Najnaj Island. It's controlled by the Saalung. It blocks the river so only a narrow channel of water can flow either side of it. This is as far as big ships can go.'

After docking, the children shuffled down the gangplank in their chains. As Tizzie stepped onto the island, she was struck by how quiet and sleepy the town seemed.

Very few people were about. And those that were visible were all moving extremely slowly.

The reason was simple. It was HOT!

Perspiration poured from Tizzie's skin.

'Bit sticky,' observed Jack, as he wiped his dripping forehead with his forearm.

'See that path over there,' said Janxa, 'on the north bank of the river, on the edge of the jungle?'

'Yes,' said Tizzie, as she looked where Janxa was pointing.

'That's where Pigleg was attacked by the big boar. Nobody else has ever survived a Grunter attack. It was such an event, there's even a stone which marks the spot. The Captain is a bit of a hero in these parts. The boar eats their children, so the locals do all they can to help him find Grunter.'

The boar eats their children…

Janxa's words were ringing in Tizzie's ears as she walked.

What must it be like to live your whole life in a place like Erthwurld?

The children were marched along the main street of Nwotegroeg in chains and then on to the outskirts of the town. Sweat poured from them all in the intense heat. Tizzie was finding it hard to breathe.

Glancing up into the trees, she saw all sorts of strange and colourful birds. A man was hauling himself up one of the trees using a raffia strap.

'He's after the palm milk,' said Janxa. 'It's sweet and delicious and fizzes when it touches your tongue.'

'I could drink ten cups of it right now,' said Tizzie. 'I'm still thirsty from eating all those salty peanuts.'

Now they came to a big enclosure. It was stocked high with all sorts of wood.

Pigleg spent a lot of money.

'Why is he buying so much wood?' asked Tizzie.

Jack was unable to enlighten her.

'Not sure. But it'll be something to do with the Grunter hunt.'

THIRTY-FIVE

Wottat

The children were made to carry all the wood that Pigleg had purchased.

On the way back to the ship, the Captain suddenly stopped.

'Now mates, after all that spendin', I'd say it's time for rum and ale while we catch up with all the news at the Jungleland Inn. All in favour, say Aye!'

'AYE CAP'N!' shouted all the men in unison.

As well as being a drinking den, the dilapidated old building was a place where visitors met locals, and all the news and gossip of Jungleland and Erthwurld were exchanged.

As they approached, Tizzie could hear drum music and singing coming from inside. The sound got louder as they got nearer.

On a walkway in front of the inn, there was a man sleeping soundly on a chair with an empty flagon of rum beside him. He looked exactly like Mr Purgy, with exactly the same tattoos.

But Purgy was clearly standing next to Gurt.

'I see your twin brother is in his usual place,' said Pigleg to Purgy. 'And in his usual state of inebriation.'

'Aye, sir, he's always been a little over-fond of his ale and rum.'

'Well, open his shirt then.'

Purgy did as he was told and opened his brother's shirt. He also opened his own shirt. His brother slept on soundly.

Now Tizzie could see that there was a living tattoo on the man's chest that looked just like Tattow. The tattoo was already awake. Its eyes were darting about – up, down, and sideways – as if it were trying to look everywhere at once.

Purgy thumped on his own chest.

'Urgh. What. Wassup?!'

Tattow woke up with his usual reluctance but seemed very pleased to see his brother.

'How's it going, bro?'

'Fine, just fine. How's it with you?'

Pigleg quickly interrupted the fraternal reunion.

'Well, Wottat, what do you know?'

'Glad to see *you* too, Cap'n.'

'I've not got the time fer pleasantries,' said Pigleg impatiently, 'just tell me the news.'

'You know the going rate for the news and gossip, Cap'n.'

Pigleg grunted his dissatisfaction. But he knew he would have to pay for news of Grunter.

'Mr Cudgel, hand me me pursebag.'

Cudgel stepped forward with Pigleg's money bag.

The Captain opened up the drawstring in the theatrical manner he always adopted when spending money. He took out one shiny gold evo very slowly and held it out in front of Wottat between two fingers, so that the talking tattoo could see clearly what it was.

'In the pocket as usual thank you, Cap'n.'

Click, thud. Click, thud. Click, thud.

Pigleg stepped onto the wooden walkway, taking three paces before leaning forward to drop the coin in a pocket of the tatty old coat worn by Purgy's snoring brother.

On receipt of the payment, Wottat began telling the news.

'The oinkroar has been heard near Crosstrails Clearing three times in the last seven days. So Grunter is in the area. The pig has taken five children already this week. They found his tracks next to the bones on the North Trail. And he has a mate... the locals call her "Saowa".'

'Another mutant?' enquired Pigleg.

'Yes indeed. And they have a family. At least six boarlets if the trackers are right.'

'Six!' exclaimed Pigleg, as if relishing the thought of more wild boars to kill. 'So we may have an even bigger scrap on our hands when it comes to it, eh mates?!'

'Aye, Cap'n,' shouted the other pirates, all shaking their fists in unison. Although it seemed to Tizzie that their enthusiasm was rather more muted than their leader's.

'And what news of the big pig and... *peanuts*?' asked the Captain.

'Grunter is taking them at every opportunity. In the last two weeks, four storage barn doors have been broken down at night. He's been stealing the nuts by the evton. Especially the salted ones. Can't resist them it seems. And the tracks at the scene suggest that his boarlets have developed a strong liking for them as well.'

'So, it's true,' mused Pigleg, 'the Grunters love peanuts. Which means the trap we've planned may just work. Any other news worth hearing about?'

Wottat continued with the news from around Erthwurld.

Tizzie was especially interested in one particular item because it was about the place where she had last seen Louis.

'Kernowland has been conquered. It's called *Wonrekland* now. And the new king, Manaccan the Merciless, has offered a reward of five thousand evos for the live capture of the boy on that poster.'

All eyes were now on the poster.

It was nailed to a post outside the inn.
Tizzie couldn't believe whose face was on it.

THIRTY-SIX

The Lumo at Lakeb

As they got halfway across the river on the ferryraft from Yaruog, Akbar spoke in a warning tone.

'That town you can see on the other side is Lakeb, which is in the Kingchiefdom of Lagenes. Stick close to me when we dock. Lakeb is notorious throughout the Empire. There are some wild people who come to the Lumoplace. It's full of muggers and pickpockets and vagabonds of all shapes and sizes.'

'But there is a worse danger. Fort Lakeb is where Governor Senega resides. He commands an Imperial Garrison. That means soldiers and secret police will be everywhere. *And* their spies. We must be careful to avoid them all. We haven't got Citizen Papers. If we're caught without papers, they'll arrest us as suspected rebels or runaway slaves.'

'Senega,' said Hans thoughtfully. 'I sink I have heard zat name before.'

'The governor is one of Evile's worst,' confirmed Akbar. 'He's particularly ruthless when it comes to rebels and runaways. Makes an example of them by stripping off their robes and hanging them up high in small cages at the Lumo. So that all the other slaves and would-be rebels can watch them shrivel to death in the sun. It's a warning not to rebel or run away.'

As Akbar was speaking, Louis imagined how horrible it must be to get caught as a rebel or a runaway and be left hanging high in a cage, shrivelling in the sun.

'I suggest we pretend that you are my slaves, then only one of us will need to talk if we're stopped.'

It was quite some way to the Lumo. When they finally arrived at the entrance to the market place, the first thing Louis saw was five men in small cages suspended high above the ground.

They all had their hands through the cage bars, and their tongues were hanging out. None of them made a sound, but it was as if they were pleading for water and mercy with their outstretched fingers.

Louis didn't know if it was because of what Akbar had said, but he suddenly felt like every soldier and secret policeman and spy was staring at him. He looked down at the ground and covered his face as much as possible with his clothes.

It was then that he saw it, or rather *them*. The posters with his own likeness on them. Everywhere.

'Zat looks like…' began Hans.

'Hold your tongue and ride on,' admonished Akbar.

Hans looked shocked to learn from the posters that little Louis was an outlaw! And a prince! And had a price of five *thousand* evos on his head!

But he obeyed Akbar's orders and stayed silent.

When they stopped to get food and other provisions for the journey to Jungleland, Akbar spoke to Hans in a whisper.

'All you need to know for now is that Louis is a rebel prince wanted for fighting against the empire, and he is completely innocent of any crime. We will tell you the whole story later. But for now we need to buy a lot of weapons, in case we have to do battle with Pigleg. And then we must get out of this town… *fast*.'

They made their purchases at the weapons stall.

As they were packing the guns and other weapons on to the

zonkeys, a man came up behind them and took a special interest in what they were doing.

'Looks like you are expecting serious trouble on your travels, friend,' he said, as if it were more of a question than a statement.

'Can't be too careful, friend,' replied Akbar. 'You never know what sort of vagabonds you might meet on the roads around here.'

'Oh, of course,' said the man, eyeing Akbar and his new weapons suspiciously. 'You can never be too careful in this region, friend.'

With that, he disappeared into the crowd as quickly and silently as he had arrived.

Louis looked around.

The hairs on the back of his neck were bristling.

It *wasn't* his imagination, he was *sure* of it. Lots of shady characters *were* watching their every move from the corners and shadowy places all around the market.

Had someone recognised him from the posters?

Had they recognised Akbar?

Did they know Hans was a runaway slave?

From the way he was looking around, Hans obviously felt the same sense of unease.

'We must leave quickly,' said Akbar. 'I don't know if my "friend" was a spy, or secret policeman, or villain.

'But his manner was all wrong.

'And, whoever he is, his type always hunts in a pack.

'So let's go…

'Now.'

THIRTY-SEVEN

Assassin!

Tizzie was in shock.

She stood as still as a statue, staring at the picture of her brother. He was strangely dressed; looking, she thought, rather grown-up in his Kernowland uniform.

On the one hand, she was happy to see he was still alive, at least at the time the poster was drawn. But, on the other hand, she was very worried by what she heard next.

'Five thousand evos for that little boy?' queried Pigleg. 'That's more than we can get for our whole cargo of children at the slave auction. What's the little villain done, then?'

'Yes, quite so, Cap'n,' said Wottat. 'It is a huge sum. Apparently he's a dangerous assassin. A rebel Prince of Forestland. He's already killed important people in Kernowland… I mean *Wonrek*land.

'They've sent messenger birds carrying reward posters all around Erthwurld. They're desperate to have him returned in time for a public execution when the Emperor visits his newly-conquered territory.'

'Interesting… *very* interesting,' said Pigleg, scratching his beard with his hook. 'So bounty hunters everywhere will be looking for 'im by now.'

'They certainly will, Cap'n,' agreed Wottat.

'For that sort of reward, we'll have to watch out for him too, eh lads?'

'Aye, Cap'n,' shouted the men in unison.

'Haharr!' guffawed Pigleg, 'with my share, I could even get Grunter's bone fused to me stump by a mutationeer, eh mates?'

'Aye, Cap'n,' laughed the men.

'But for now, we've got some more revellin' to do,' continued Pigleg.

'YAYYY!' cheered the men.

'Gurt, take the slavelings back to the ship. We're going to party!'

'Gurrhhhh,' gurgled Gurt, nodding his head as he did so.

Thwcrack!

The children had to carry all the wood and other provisions back to the ship with Gurt cracking Lasher every few steps to make sure they all stayed in line.

Thwcrack!

Thwcrack!

By the time they got there, sweat was pouring from their pores as they dumped their loads into a roped-off area on the dock.

Thwcrack!

Thwcrack!

Lasher cracked again and again as they trudged up the gangplank onto the ship and descended the steps into the hold.

Tizzie laid her head on her rag pillow and closed her eyes.

But, exhausted as she was, she found it particularly difficult to get to sleep. All the things Wottat had said about her little brother, Louis, were going around and around in her head.

Bounty Hunters.

Reward.

Prince.

Rebel.

Assassin!

What *had* Louis been up to?

THIRTY-EIGHT

Bounty Hunters

Louis and his companions left Lakeb in a hurry.

As they rode their zonkeys speedily away, Akbar outlined the plan.

'We will be heading south-east, towards the town of Adnuocabmat. From there it is only a short ride on the jungle trail to the rendezvous point I suggested to the rebels in my note. It's near Ofeneug, a village on the River Aibmag.'

At intervals throughout the climb into the steep hills of the Little Mountains, Akbar had been looking behind at regular intervals. Then he spotted them.

'Pursuers.'

All three companions now looked behind.

'Ten riders. Our "friend" is with them. I think he may have recognised you, Louis.'

They all thought the same thing at the same time.

Bounty hunters!

Bang!

Pzzzzzzzzzttt!

A shot narrowly missed Akbar's head.

'Amateurs!' said the warrior sheik, dismissively. 'They have shown their intentions far too soon. But they are still ten and we are only three. We need to reach the high ground.'

Louis thought he knew why. Then Akbar confirmed that he was right.

'There a few can defend against many. If we can find the right spot, we three will soon dispense with that pack of manwolves. The hunters will become the hunted.'

Louis kicked his heels into Faloo's flank to make the little zonkey go faster.

Bang!

Pzzzzzzzzzttt!

Bang!

Pzzzzzzzzzttt!

Shots rang out and bullets whizzed by at intervals as they climbed. Swirls of dust and scattering stones marked their ascent up the hillside.

The young boy could hear a repeating refrain in his head as they fled.

'*This is such hard work... This is such hard work... This is such hard work...*'

But he couldn't be kind to the zonkey and stop kicking.

This was a life-or-death situation for them all.

'Sorry, Faloo, but we must climb fast. They may kill you too.'

'*This is easier than I thought... This is easier than I thought...*'

THIRTY-NINE

Grunter Territory

Next morning, after a breakfast of salted peanuts, Tizzie and the other children were marched down the gangplank and lined up on the dock.

Was today the day they would be boar bait?

A cart was waiting there. It had the huge barrel they'd collected in Ruatnuk loaded on the back.

A sad looking zonkey was harnessed to the front of the cart. Tizzie felt sorry for the little zonkey having to pull such a heavy load.

'Right,' said Purgy, 'pick up all the supplies you can carry.'

'Gurt... no shirkers.'

'Gurrhhhh!'

Thwcrack!

Thwcrack!

Lasher cracked twice to let the children know they shouldn't shirk.

Tizzie and the other children did as they were told – one helping another to tie a heavy bundle on their backs – each fearful of the consequences should they not be loaded up with the most they could manage.

'Now follow me, follow me.'

Again the children did as they were told.

'Gurt, keep 'em in line.'

Gurrhhhh!

Thwcrack!

With Purgy leading, and Gurt cracking Lasher as he moved alongside them, the children set out in single file from the dock.

Big Bessie was bustling off in the opposite direction.

'Jenny said she's visiting her grandmother,' said Jack.

Four other pirates – armed with muskets – and two local Saalung guides had joined them at the dock, and they now walked with the children.

Bent almost double by the load on her back, Tizzie strained her neck upwards to look ahead. They were heading towards a bridge on the north side of Najnaj Island.

The heavily-laden children padded slowly over the bridge towards the mainland. When they got to the other side, they turned right and marched a little way along the path by the side of the river.

They soon came to a sign on the path. It was pointing north along a trail which led straight into the dense jungle.

Tizzie read the sign: 'South Trail'.

'Protection squad… muskets *ready*,' said Purgy.

Tizzie could hear the fear in his voice. If *Purgy* was scared, something in that jungle must be *really* dangerous.

The musketmen raised their weapons, in apparent readiness to fire at whatever it was that seemed to be scaring the tough Mr Purgy so much.

The tattooed pirate took a tentative step onto the trail and led them into the jungle.

Janxa spoke in a whisper.

'Looks like they're taking us to Crosstrails Clearing.'

Tizzie heard what Jack whispered back in a grave tone.

'Grunter territory.'

FORTY

Lioneagles

High in the Little Mountains, Akbar chose a place to make a stand.

'Here, get in position behind these rocks.'

Louis and Hans did as they were told and listened to their leader's orders.

'We'll all fire at once when they come round the bend and reach that tree down there.'

Like Louis, Akbar had read the instructions on the cataball ammo belt.

'Louis, you fire your catapult. A yellow ball. Right into the middle of them. Hans, aim at the lead rider with your pistol. I'll take the last man with my riflemusket.

'But wait until I give the signal. We mustn't fire until they've all come around the bend and the last man has reached the tree.'

'Okay,' said Louis.

Thoump! Thoump! Thoump!

He was trying to be brave but his heart was beating very fast and his hand shook as he picked out a yellow cataball.

'Right,' said Hans, in a deep voice as if he was tough and grown-up. But Louis could see in his demeanour that he was very scared too.

Louis waited behind the rock, trembling more and more uncontrollably by the second as he imagined what might happen next.

All too quickly, it was time.

Making sure he stayed out of sight, he watched from behind his rock as the first man came around the bend.

He waited.

Hans waited.

Akbar waited.

Finally, the last man had reached the tree.

'FIRE!' shouted Akbar.

Fzzzzzzzzzzzzzzzzzzzzzzzzzzz!

Louis fired into the middle of the bandits.

Psssshhhhhhhhhh!

Hans fired his pistol at the lead rider.

Ptsssssssssssssssssss!

Akbar fired his riflemusket at the last rider.

Down by the tree, the first and last rider fell.

TWWWWWRRRRRRRRRRRRR!

At the same time, the eight other riders were all taken completely by surprise by the swirling twister released from the yellow cataball as it hit the ground and expanded in their midst.

The whirling wind extended to a diameter of ten paces in an instant and span around for twelve seconds, knocking them from their mounts and scattering them in all directions before ceasing as quickly as it had begun.

The eight startled men scrambled to their feet, firing randomly into the surrounding hills as they did so.

Bang!

Pzzzzzzzzzzttt!

Bang!

Pzzzzzzzzzzttt!

Bang!

Pzzzzzzzzzttt!

Shots whizzed by as Louis hid behind the rock and fumbled for another cataball.

Which one should he fire now?

Akbar hadn't said.

'Loarrrrrrrrrrrrrrrrrrrrrrrrrrrrr!'

'Loarrrrrrrrrrrrrrrrrrrrrrrrrrrr!'

'Loarrrrrrrrrrrrrrrrrrrrrrrrrrrr!'

Suddenly, there was a roaring from the air.

Louis looked up to see the source of the terrifying sound.

About a dozen or so winged creatures were diving down towards the bounty hunters.

They were mutant monsters.

They had flowing manes and feathered wings.

And huge outstretched talons.

'Lioneagles!' exclaimed Hans in terror and awe.

FORTY-ONE

Crosstrails Clearing

'Where is Crosstrails Clearing?' asked Tizzie, when they had stopped for a break.

'It's in the middle of the jungle,' answered Jack.

'Eight trails fan out from it.

'The North Trail leads north.

'Then there's a trail heading north-east.

'Another heads east.

'Then south-east.

'Then the South Trail leads south and so on around the rest of the eight main points of the compass.

'At the moment we're heading north on the South Trail.'

'Is there something special at the clearing?' asked Tizzie.

'No, there's nothing there except a big open circle where the trees have been cut down and the other vegetation has been cleared away,' answered Janxa.

'But it's *the* major crossroads in Jungleland. It links up lots of the main places.'

'And everybody uses it to get from one place to another by land,' added Jack, 'unless it makes more sense to use the river.'

'Come on, come on, no slacking, no slacking,' said Purgy as he made the children stand in line again after their short break.

'Gurt, we need to get to the clearing well before dusk tomorrow.

'The Cap'n wants everything ready when he arrives.

'Follow me…
'And make them pick up the pace.'
'Gurrhhhh!'
Thwcrack!
'Sounds like Pigleg and the others will be coming to the clearing after we get there tomorrow,' said Jack, as he strained to take the weight of his heavy burden before setting out at marching pace once more.

Tizzie was left wondering something…

So why are *we* going today?

FORTY-TWO

The Edge of Jungleland

'Loarrrrrrrrrrrrrrrrrrrrrrrrrrrrrr!'

'Cease fire,' shouted Akbar as the pride of lioneagles tore into the bandits with their talons and teeth.

'Argghhhhhhhhhhhh!'

'Nohhhhhhhhhhh!'

Bang!

Pzzzzzzzzzttt!

The men screamed and fought and some fired their weapons but they had no chance against such terrifying beasts.

'Argghhhhhhhhhhh!'

'Nohhhhhhhhhhh!'

The attack by the flying carnivores was ferocious.

It was horrible to watch.

Louis stared, rooted to the spot by fear.

'Now's our chance, we must GO!' said Akbar, with great urgency in his voice.

Louis didn't move.

'I said NOW!' said Akbar, as he grabbed Louis' arm and pulled him towards their zonkeys.

Louis was brought back to the moment. He ran, jumped into his saddle, kicked his heels hard into Faloo's flanks, and rode as fast as he could to the sound of a panting voice in his head.

'*Lioneagles!*

'*Got to get away... Got to get away... Got to get away...*'

Hans and Akbar followed and soon they were descending the slopes on the southern side of the Little Mountains at a rapid pace.

When they had put a good distance between themselves and the scene of the attack, Akbar signalled that it was safe to slow down.

'Lioneagles are a great danger in this region. I must, however, admit that I was rather glad to see them! But it is still likely that we would have defeated the bounty hunters on our own. So, well done back there, young warriors. You kept your heads and followed orders. And you both showed courage. I am proud to ride with you.'

Louis and Hans looked at each other and smiled.

They were very pleased to hear Akbar's words. Praise from a man such as him meant a great deal to both of them.

'I think, now that we've got our provisions and weapons, we'll avoid visiting any more towns,' continued the sheik. 'There is no need to go through Adnuocabmat. It is true that going along the road through the town would be the easier route, but considering we are without papers – and with those posters everywhere – I think it would be advisable to leave the road just before we get to the town.'

Louis and Hans nodded and followed their leader as he led the way. They both acknowledged that he knew much more about what was a good thing to do than they did.

It wasn't long before they had Adnuocabmat in sight.

'There's the town ahead,' said Akbar. 'We need to head south.'

They skirted around the southern edge without incident.

Late in the afternoon Louis lifted his head to look ahead.

About one kilom in the distance lay a lush, green forest.

'We have made good time,' said Akbar.

'That's the edge of Jungleland.'

FORTY-THREE

Rendezvous With The Rebels

Akbar, Hans, and Louis rode under an archway of branches.

They had crossed into Jungleland.

Louis looked up into the canopy, and then forward along the trail. It was as if they were travelling down a tunnel of trees.

He wondered what lay ahead.

'Weapons ready,' said Akbar. 'We could be attacked by all manner of carnivorous beasts at any moment. There are some particularly ferocious chewing creatures in this jungle.'

Louis' heart began to beat faster with every word as Akbar continued. 'Make no sound unless absolutely necessary. And stay vigilant at all times.'

Louis' senses went in to overdrive as they travelled deeper into the jungle. His ears listened for the slightest sound of danger and his eyes constantly scanned the trees.

At dusk, Akbar spoke again.

'The River Aibmag is only a short distance ahead. We will soon be at the rendezvou…'

Ftttttttttttttttttttt!

Ftttttttttttttttttttt!

Two arrows hit the jungle trail in front of the sheik's zonkey, stopping him in his tracks.

'There are six of us. We have you surrounded. Drop your weapons and put your hands in the air,' instructed a voice from the trees.

With that, six Blackskin Acirfan men appeared as if from nowhere, their weapons pointed at the three travellers.

'Who do we owe?' asked the tallest Acirfan, looking straight at Akbar.

'Clevercloggs the Explorer,' said Akbar.

The men now smiled.

'Greetings, Rebels of Sandland,' said the tall man. 'I am Yoro Jilla.'

'Greetings, Rebels of Jungleland. I am Akbar Sharif.'

'My aunt, Joyous, also sends her greetings to you all,' said Yoro. 'She got your message and immediately sent us to help you. We have been waiting.'

Louis had been watching and listening with interest. He now saw that the question and answer was a test to confirm identity on both sides.

The young boy listened carefully as Akbar then explained more to the men about their quest to rescue Tizzie.

At one point, the warrior sheik borrowed *Zoomer* and showed them how it worked with *Rescuer*, the space orbiter.

Yoro and the other men – and especially Hans – all seemed fascinated.

'Here is Pigleg's ship, *The Revenger*,' said Akbar as he zoomed in for the men to see. It seems he is at Nwotegroeg already!'

'Yes, we've seen him,' confirmed Yoro. 'I had heard stories about the speed and size of those whalehorses but had never seen one in the flesh until Pigleg arrived at Janjan Island. He and his men have been partying at the Jungleland Inn. That's how we know what their plans are.'

From the reactions of Akbar, Hans, and the Acirfans to his zooming map, Louis could see that new technology from

Kernowland's Goonhilly inventing facility was of real interest to people from all over Erthwurld.

Then Yoro expressed a concern which worried Louis too.

'This *Zoomer* is very clever. But now that Evile has taken Kernowland and made it Wonrekland, he will now have access to this technology. If he can make more of them, the eyes in the skies will allow him to spy on everybody, everywhere, all the time.'

'Precisely,' agreed Akbar, 'It will make him much more powerful and he may even be able to extinguish all resistance. Which makes it imperative that we find a way to stop Evile once and for all, before he makes Erthwurld an even more terrible place for our children to grow up in.'

'We agree,' said Yoro solemnly. 'But for now, I will tell you what I know so that we can get on with the rescue.'

Louis listened carefully again as Yoro brought them up-to-date with his news.

'We have learned that Pigleg plans to set a trap at Crosstrails Clearing using peanuts and childbait. As well as the princess girl you seek, he has some of our children too. More of our people will be at the clearing to help when the time comes.'

Louis thought this was very good news as Yoro continued with some surprising information.

'And Clevercloggs himself will be there too. He is already in Jungleland, with two others. He has made contact with my aunt, saying that he is here to rescue the princess. We have replied and told him where she will be.'

'Is Mr Sand one of the people with Clevercloggs?' interrupted Louis, unable to stop himself.

'I am very sorry, but I do not know,' answered Yoro.

'Clevercloggs is far too experienced to write down all the names in a note, in case it got intercepted. We only knew it was him because he used the secret code.'

Louis allowed himself a glimmer of hope that Mr Sand had survived and come through the Crystal Door as they had planned.

'Follow us,' said Yoro, 'we have canoes at the river.'

With that, they all set out heading south on the trail.

When they got to the river, they unloaded all the supplies and weapons and freed the zonkeys. Faloo and the other four pack animals cantered off back down the trail.

'Bye-bye, Faloo,' waved Louis. He had grown a little attached to his lazy mount, and hoped the little zonkey and his friends would get out of the jungle safely.

'Where are ze canoes?' asked Hans.

'Hidden,' answered Yoro. 'We cannot just leave them openly on the riverbank. They may be stolen, and we don't want to attract attention from the trail patrols.'

He and his men then pulled back some hanging branches, which had camouflaged the canoes very effectively.

Louis looked at the boats. They were made from long, dugout tree trunks.

'As the river flows from the high hills to the low plains on its journey towards the sea,' explained Akbar, 'there are rapids and waterfalls along the way. These men are experts at navigating the river, which is by far the fastest way to move around Jungleland. We will use the canoes to take us almost as far as Nwotegroeg. Then we'll travel inland to Crosstrails Clearing. The canoes have to be small, in order that they can be carried along the river paths past the waterfalls and any other natural obstacles.'

Louis glanced at the dugout canoes again. They didn't look

that small to him. In fact they looked far too heavy for a young boy like him to carry.

Louis stepped into one canoe. It wobbled wildly from side to side. He sat down quickly and grabbed the sides with his hands as Akbar and Hans stepped into the second and third canoes.

Three leaf-shaped oarpaddles lay on the bottom of the boat.

Two of the Bulubaa men then got into the canoe with Louis, one at each end. They began propelling the canoe forward, each using one of the oarpaddles with both hands. Louis just sat there, enjoying the ride.

After a few moments, the man at the front turned his head and frowned at Louis with a disgusted look on his face.

'Paddle then, boy. Prince of Forestland or not, everyone must pull their weight in a Bulubaa canoe.'

Louis quickly grabbed up the third oarpaddle, embarrassed that the men thought he was not paddling because he was a spoiled prince.

But the embarrassment soon passed as he got the hang of paddling with the oarpaddle.

The young boy looked ahead with a good feeling inside.

At last he felt he truly had a chance of rescuing Tizzie.

FORTY-FOUR

The Roll Of Death

As Louis paddled, he looked at all the animals in the water and along the banks of the river.

Nobody was telling him what all the different mixed up mutants were, so he tried to guess what they might be called.

Some of his guesses were 'badgerbat', 'hyenaporcupine', and 'catsnake', though he wasn't at all sure he'd got the mixes right.

After a little while, the men in his boat seemed to have forgotten about his mistake with the oarpaddle and started talking to him.

'I am Nfansu, son of Kanimang and Nyima,' said the man at the front.

'I am Bakary, son of Momodou and Sukai,' said the man at the back.

'I am Louis, son of Robert and Veronica,' said Louis.

Now they had all been introduced, the men seemed very friendly. At first they told him about the river and how important it was for the people of Jungleland, especially for transport and food. Then they told him about some of the animals.

'There's a kingfisherbat,' said Nfansu.

'Look at him dive,' added Bakary with real admiration, as the batbird hit the water at incredible speed.

'And he's got a fish in his beak!' exclaimed Louis a moment later.

The wide-eyed boy was really enjoying learning about the river and the animals of Jungleland from his new friends. Until they started telling him about something not so nice. A chewing creature that lived and hunted in the river.

'There is a beast that we are all taught to fear as young children,' began Bakary. 'It is the river's most dangerous carnivore.'

'The monster has a huge fat body, thick skin that repels a spear, and huge long jaws with seventy or more pointed teeth,' added Nfansu. 'It lies in wait and then attacks without warning, turning over your boat and tipping you into the water.'

'The main reason we fear them is the way they kill you,' said Bakary. 'They have a special technique for killing their prey. It's called the *roll of death*.'

'Yes,' continued Nfansu, 'they lock on tight with their jaws, and then roll you around and around under the water, bruising your flesh, ripping off chunks, and breaking your bones on rocks in the process.'

'That's how they tenderise you,' added Bakary.

'What does tenderise mean?' asked Louis, not certain that he really wanted to know.

'It means making you softer to eat,' answered Nfansu. 'They like their meat soft – rotten and putrid – like an over-ripe peach.'

'One of them ate my grandfather,' said Bakary, with genuine dread in his voice. 'Wedged him under a rock beneath the water after the death roll… and fed on him for days afterwards.'

Louis thought this was just *a bit too much* information to be giving a little boy, but he was now absolutely itching to know the name of the beast that struck such fear in the hearts of the Bulubaa.

'What's the monster called?'

'The long-jawed crocoppotamus.'

FORTY-FIVE

Whitewater Alley

Night was closing in on the river.

'We will camp tonight on the south bank,' said Bakary. 'It is not safe for us to stay on the north side of the river. Empire troops and Saalung slavers patrol the trails.'

'And there may be bounty hunters who have seen the posters in town as well,' warned Nfansu. 'Prince Louis has a high price on his head and many a villain would travel far and wide for five thousand evos.'

Louis didn't know whether to be flattered or concerned that so many people might be looking for him.

When they stopped, he tried to help lift the canoe onto the riverbank. It was very heavy and he didn't think he'd contributed very much to getting it out of the water. The men did, however, seem to appreciate his trying, and they even entrusted him with the job of hiding the canoe.

'Very good,' praised Nfansu after he had finished. 'Nobody would know it is there.'

They made camp.

'It will be a hard day tomorrow,' said Yoro around the fire. 'We have to canoe the rapids.'

That night, Louis found it difficult to get to sleep. He was excited but at the same time scared by the thought of canoeing through rapids tomorrow. In the end, the fact that he was completely worn out meant that he at least got a few hours rest.

'Tseeep!' 'Tseeep!' 'Tseeep!'

'Vvit!' 'Vvit!' 'Vvit!'

'Cheweeweewee!' 'Cheweeweewee!' 'Cheweeweewee!'

The Jungleland Dawn Chorus woke them in the morning.

The Bulubaa had brought some food.

For breakfast, there was only enough for everyone to have one raw pigchicken egg each and a little geep's milk.

Louis didn't complain. He was glad to be eating something nutritious and knew he had to have whatever was on offer. Whether he liked the thought or taste of the food wasn't as important as surviving long enough to rescue Tizzie. He was growing tougher by the hour in this dangerous place.

They were soon setting off in the canoes once more.

Louis was happy to be with his two new friends again.

'When do we get to the rapids?' he asked.

'Not long now,' answered Nfansu, 'but I wouldn't be looking forward to it if I were you.'

'You will know the rapids are close when the water starts flowing faster,' said Bakary.

'Why does it do that?' asked Louis.

'Because,' answered Nfansu, 'although the river is now flowing on quite flat terrain through the high plateau, the land will soon start sloping down.'

'The river speeds up as it flows through the sloping land,' added Bakary.

'Then, when the fast-flowing water hits rocks on the river bed, it becomes agitated, and the foaming white rapids are created,' said Nfansu.

'It's called *Whitewater Alley*,' said Bakary.

'The alley is about two kiloms long,' continued Nfansu.

'And it's the most dangerous part of the river before the falls.'

'The *falls*!' gulped Louis.

'Yes, *Cascade Falls*,' said Bakary. 'After Whitewater Alley, there's about half a kilom of slower flowing water – called *Last Chance Run* – and then the river reaches the edge of the plateau, with nowhere to go but straight down.'

'It's a very steep drop over sheer rock to the plains below,' added Nfansu. 'No one has ever survived going over the edge as far as we know.'

'So how do we stop going over Cascade Falls with the canoes?' asked Louis, sincerely hoping that his friends knew the answer.

'We need strong paddling to bank the canoes when we get to the Last Chance Run,' answered Bakary. 'And then we can carry them down the Cascade Trail to the lower ground, where we join the river again.'

'But the only trouble is…' began Nfansu.

Louis couldn't believe it; after all that to worry about, there was something else.

'…the Last Chance Run is one of the places where the crocoppotamuses like to swim. There's a whole bloat of them there sometimes.'

'Bloat?' queried Louis.

'That's what a group of them is called.'

'Oh, I see.'

'And, the last I heard, Bullcroc and his bloat are there at the moment,' added Nfansu. 'If that's true, we're in real trouble.'

'Yes,' agreed Bakary. 'The males are very territorial, and canoes floating through their stretch of river can make them very angry. Bullcroc is the worst of them, a huge bad-tempered specimen. So, if given the choice, I'd rather not take the chance.'

'But we have no choice,' said Nfansu. 'We must navigate this river if we are to get to the Crosstrails Clearing as fast as possible.'

'Yes,' agreed Bakary, 'our children and your sister will surely be eaten by Grunter if we can't get there in time to save them.'

With that thought in mind, Louis and his companions canoed on down the river as fast as they could go.

Then, as they rounded a bend in the river, the young boy saw it…

'Whitewater Alley!' shouted Bakary.

The raging rapids were less than a kilom ahead.

Nfansu, who was at the front of the canoe, gave Louis instructions.

'If I say, "steer right", put your oarpaddle in the water as deep as you can on this side of the canoe like this. If I say, "steer left", do the same on the other side.'

As they got nearer to the rapids, Louis noticed the frothing, bubbling sound. And he felt the increase in speed as the water began to push the canoe along much faster.

Without warning, Nfansu shouted at the top of his voice.

'STEER LEFT!'

They narrowly missed the first huge boulder. Louis' oarpaddle scraped the stone as they shot past it.

Suddenly, they were *in* the rapids.

They had entered Whitewater Alley. The canoe immediately picked up lots more speed. Louis was bounced and thrown about as the canoe yawed and pitched and rolled.

'Right!
'Left!
'Right!
'Right'

Nfansu now omitted the 'steer' part of the instruction as the boulders filled the river ahead. There wasn't time to say it.

The force of the water was incredible. Louis found that just keeping the oarpaddle in the water was hugely difficult.

Following on behind, the other two crews were having equal trouble navigating the raging rapids.

Then, as quickly as the foaming torrent had begun, it ceased.

The three crews had successfully navigated Whitewater Alley.

But their troubles were by no means over.

They had entered Last Chance Run.

FORTY-SIX

Carnivorous Crocoppotamuses

By comparison, everything in Last Chance Run seemed very quiet. The water was still flowing quite quickly, but it was a gentle stream compared to The Alley.

'Paddle quietly, slowly, and gently,' advised Bakary.

'Yes, best not to disturb them if they're here,' added Nfansu.

Louis paddled very quietly indeed.

'We'll bank the canoes over there where the Cascade Trail starts,' whispered Nfansu.

All three canoes headed for the place where he was pointing.

When they were nearly at the river bank, Bakary laughed and joked.

'Well, Nfansu, so much for Bullcroc and his bloat being here. Looks like you heard wron...'

Suddenly, right in the middle of his sentence, the canoe was lifted out of the water at the stern end.

'Aaaaaaaaaaargghhhhhhhhhhhhhhhh!'

'Aaaaaaaaaaargghhhhhhhhhhhhhhhh!'

'Aaaaaaaaaaargghhhhhhhhhhhhhhhh!'

Screaming loudly, Louis, Bakary, and Nfansu were thrown from the canoe as it turned upside down.

'BULLCROC!'

'Aaaaaaaaaaargghhhhhhhhhhhhhhhh!'

'Aaaaaaaaaaargghhhhhhhhhhhhhhhh!'

'Aaaaaaaaaaargghhhhhhhhhhhhhhhh!'

Everything seemed to be happening in slow motion. Louis heard more screams from the other boats as he travelled through the air.

'Aaaaaaaaaargghhhhhhhhhhhhhhhh!'

'Aaaaaaaaaargghhhhhhhhhhhhhhhh!'

'Aaaaaaaaaargghhhhhhhhhhhhhhhh!'

Flplash!

The young boy hit the water with a belly-flop.

He was still holding on to his oarpaddle.

His head was under the water.

He opened his eyes. Nothing could have prepared the terrified young boy for what he saw beneath the surface.

A huge creature, part crocodile and part hippopotamus, was coming straight towards him. Its big pink-red mouth was open wide.

There were two rows of jagged teeth set in long jaws.

As Louis let go of the oarpaddle and turned to swim for his life, Akbar was suddenly at his side, with dagger drawn.

Bullcroc was only feet away, bearing down on them fast.

Akbar grabbed Louis' oarpaddle and put himself between boy and beast. The huge chewing creature brought its jaws together.

The brave sheik wedged the oarpaddle in the monster's mouth and stuck his dagger deep into its tongue.

But the creature was too big and its jaws too strong for one man with a paddle and a dagger, however brave the man.

The oarpaddle snapped and the jaws closed.

A cloud of muddy sediment formed in the water as the huge beast began the roll of death.

'Nohhhhhhhhhhhhhhhh!'

Louis yelled, as if trying to stop what was happening.

But however loud he cried, he couldn't stop it.

Akbar was gone.

FORTY-SEVEN

Godolphin's Map

The rest of Bullcroc's bloat – seven other huge crocoppotamuses – now joined in the attack. One of the beasts was bearing down on Louis from only a few yards away.

'Glgg. Glgg. Glgg.'

Louis was so frightened that he swallowed glug after glug of the cloudy water. He coughed and spluttered and choked as he tried to say afloat.

The monster was almost upon him.

The little boy closed his eyes and waited for the end.

Grbbb.

Suddenly, Louis felt a strong hand grab his shoulder.

Tggg.

Then a sharp tug.

He was pulled backwards through the water.

And then up on to the riverbank.

'Hans!'

Somehow, the strong youth had swum to safety. Then he had waded back into the water, grabbed Louis, and pulled him out of the water and away from the beast's charge.

Ignoring Louis for the moment, Hans now waded back into the water once more, to see if he could save anyone else.

After scanning the surface for a few moments, he returned to the riverbank, shaking his head to tell Louis that everyone was gone.

Splishhhhhhhh!

Splashhhhhhhh!

Sploshhhhhhhh!

Suddenly, before Hans or Louis could speak, there were sounds from the river.

Louis watched in terror as Bullcroc and his bloat rose out of the water once more. This time, it was obvious the chewing creatures intended to attack them on the riverbank.

'Qvickly, into ze trees.'

Louis jumped to his feet and ran. Hans ran.

The chewing creatures chased them.

The monsters were gaining fast.

Luckily, the trees were close.

The crocoppotamuses were far too big to enter the dense jungle. Once deep in the safety of the trees, Hans and Louis assessed their situation.

It seemed dire. No adults, no canoes, no provisions.

And no way of finding their way to Crosstrails Clearing.

'Vun step at a time,' said Hans. 'Let's follow ze Cascade Trail.'

Louis agreed and they set out.

The trail wound down beside the waterfall. It was so steep in places that Louis thought he would plunge right down to the ground if he slipped. It was going to take a long time to get safely to the bottom of the rock face.

Much later, they were looking up and marvelling at the sheer majesty of the Cascade Falls. And the sheer drop! They were very relieved, and somewhat amazed, that they'd got down without injury.

They followed the trail along the river. It was a solemn walk. Neither boy spoke for a long time. Both were thinking of lost friends.

Louis couldn't help thinking about the possibility of losing Tizzie. This made him even more determined to try to rescue her.

But events seemed to be going against the brave young boy.

Zoomer, his Kernow cape, and his uniform jacket had all gone over the waterfall with the canoes.

Everything was just so terrible he tried to blot all these thoughts out of his mind as he walked.

When Louis was so tired he just couldn't take another step, they stopped and made camp.

Hans caught a fish whilst Louis gathered sticks for a fire.

'Ze river is ze fastest vay to travel if you have a canoe,' said Hans as they ate. 'But it snakes and vinds, so it vill be a much longer route if ve valk beside it than it vould be if ve headed straight for ze clearing. In my own country, I can find my vay with landmarks, but in zis jungle, it is hard to know vhere you are going.'

Louis then suddenly remembered something.

'I have this.'

With that, he pulled out the Kernow Compass which was still hanging from a cord around his neck.

'Zat is gut! Very gut!' said Hans excitedly, as he took the compass in his hand and studied it. 'Anysing else?'

'Just this map my friend, Mr Sand, gave me,' said Louis, as he took the old and tattered piece of parchment from his pocket and chucked it on the ground. 'But it's a map of Kernowland, so it won't be any use here.'

'Iss zat vot I sink it iss?' said Hans, eyeing the parchment with a look of awe.

'What?' said Louis.

Hans grabbed up the map.

'Yes! A *Godolphin Map*!'

Louis looked at the map with renewed interest.

'Cool magic,' said Hans as if he thought Louis had something really special. 'Didn't you know vot it vos?'

'No,' said Louis.

'It changes to ze country you're in.'

Louis looked at the map. There was a completely different drawing on the parchment and the name had changed at the top…

… *JUNGLELAND*.

'Zeese maps are very rare and valuable,' said Hans. 'Zis Mr Sand, he must be a *very* gut friend to give you such a gift.'

'Yes,' said Louis, remembering Mr Sand fondly.

The old man was very wise. Perhaps he had given Louis the map because he knew they could be separated and Louis might need it to find his way around Erthwurld.

Zoomer was a map based on modern technology, very clever but limited to what the scientists at Goonhilly had been able to invent. But the Godolphin Map, that was something extra special. It was based on ancient knowledge and had the magical power to change as needed.

After reflecting on all this, Louis thought he'd better show Hans the other tool Mr Sand had given him. He took off the Kaski belt and handed it to the youth from the Spla Mountains.

Hans read the instructions and smiled at Louis admiringly.

'A Kernow Compass, a Godolphin Map *and* a Kaski! Ze complete jungle survival kit. You really are full of ze surprises, *Prince* Louis.'

Louis shrugged and smiled back as Hans continued.

'With zeese tools ve vill be able to get to Crosstrails Clearing by ze shortest possible route…

'A straight line!'

FORTY-EIGHT

Lister's Choice

Kernowland's change of name to Wonrekland was just one of many changes in the little kingdom since the invasion.

In order that all the people knew what was going on, Manaccan – who understood the power and importance of the media – made sure that these changes were reported in the main newspaper, *The Daily Packet*.

Under the provisions of the martial law he had imposed, the newspaper was now under his complete editorial control, and he had wasted no time in using it for propaganda purposes.

Mr Lister, the new editor, had been instructed to publish lists in order to inform the people of things that had happened or were going to happen.

It had been some time since the Banquet of Peace and Manaccan had decided that he and the warlords now had sufficient control of the kingdom to list, for the benefit of the whole population, the ten edicts that had previously only been read out to the small group who had attended the banquet.

The article explained what these new *Imperial Laws* would mean for the citizens of the new empire territory of Wonrekland.

It was particularly precise in respect of *Edict Number I*:

> *For those families with multiple*
> *children aged twelve years or*
> *younger, parents have **two weeks***

*from today to choose which one of
them is to be given into slavery.
The name of the chosen child shall
be submitted to the Office of the
Counterupper within that time, or
his representatives will be calling
at homes to make the choice on
parents' behalf.*

Although all the parents knew that the King's Counterupper hadn't actually *made* the *Edict Number I* law, it was he who had written it down, and his office that was collating the list of slavechildren chosen.

So it was that parents everywhere came to associate him with the new law and were soon referring to the agonizing decision they were being forced to make by another name...

Lister's Choice.

FORTY-NINE

Buzzing Bugs And Biting Beasties

Tizzie and the other slaves trudged north along the South Trail. It was hard work carrying such a heavy load and marching at such a fast pace.

The sights and sounds of the jungle suggested perils with every step. It was a bit like the jungle she'd seen on the television. But the bugs and beasties seemed a lot bigger, noisier, and above all, scarier, than anything she had ever seen or heard.

First she had spotted a giant termite mound. Each of the termites was the size of her thumb. Tizzie may have been scared by what she saw around her, but Yang was having great fun, seeing how many mutant insects he could spot.

'Marching ants! Look at those beautiful beasties. They're carnivores, travelling in groups of up to a quarter of a million individuals. They work as a team, foraging in fan-shaped swarms that span several paces across. That's why people call them, "swarm raiders". The swarm is like a moving, stinging blanket. It acts as one organism, a relentless killing, eating machine. The ants subdue small prey with powerful stings, and then pull off their legs and antennae using their mandibles. They carry their catch home to their nest to feed their young. Acting together, they can kill bigger food too. They take lizards, snakes, pigs, goats, scorpions, and even birds. And they've even been known to take small children when they're asleep.'

Tizzie could have done without more of Yang's enthusiastic

lesson about the army of gigantic ants that were filing past them in the opposite direction. But he was in full flow and enjoying himself.

'It must be so awful. They sting you all over first, and then, when you can't move, they...

'Yang, that's enough,' said Jack, seeing that some of the younger ones definitely didn't want to hear another word about carnivorous army ants. 'Wouldn't you like to tell us about the nice colourful birds up there?'

'No thanks,' said Yang, with a disappointed expression on his face. 'I'll just look from now on.'

In the early evening, Mr Purgy decided it was time to stop for the night. Tizzie was so pleased to rest that she didn't even mind that it was only peanuts again for dinner. She had been carrying her heavy load all day and was absolutely exhausted.

They moved off the trail a little way and built a jungle camp. This involved cutting off branches and making a temporary fortress to protect them all against the carnivorous wild animals that lived in the jungle.

'A wall of branches may keep out most of the animals but it won't protect us against a chewing creature like Grunter,' said one of the pirates.

'No, that's true enough,' said Purgy, thoughtfully. 'Get some more wood for the fire. We'll keep it going all night. And we'll just have to hope that the big boar and his brood have already eaten.'

'Tseeep!' 'Tseeep!' 'Tseeep!'

'Vvit!' 'Vvit!' 'Vvit!'

'Cheweeweewee!' 'Cheweeweewee!' 'Cheweeweewee!'

As Tizzie lay down to sleep, the birds began their familiar chirruping and squawking.

'Waaarp!' 'Waaarp!' 'Waaarp!'

'Hoahoah!' 'Hoahoah!' 'Hoahoah!'

'Yuuuur!' 'Yuuuur!' 'Yuuuur!'

Then the beasts of the jungle joined the birds.

'Ah, the Jungleland Dusk Chorus,' said Yang, forgetting Jack's earlier admonishment.

'That loud *yuuuur* is the hyenajackal. They can't manage prey the size of adults but there have been lots of stories about them taking young children in the night. Good job we've got the fire.'

'They're just stories,' said Jack, glaring at Yang for scaring the little ones again.

As the other animals and birds quietened down, the sound of one particular insect just wouldn't stop.

'Bzzzrrrbzzzrrrbzzzrrrbzzzrrrbzzzrrrbzzzrrrbzzzrrr…'

It was like a constant buzzing drill emanating from every direction.

And it was really, *really* LOUD!

'Cicadaflies,' said Janxa.

'Yes, the word cicada means 'buzzer' in Nital, the ancient language of Emor,' confirmed Yang.

There seemed no containing his enthusiasm.

'But most people call them buzzing bugs.'

Although interesting, this particular piece of information did nothing to help Tizzie sleep.

'Bzzzrrrbzzzrrrbzzzrrrbzzzrrrbzzzrrrbzzzrrr…'

Buzzer!

They certainly live up to their name, she thought, as she turned over to try to get comfortable on the bed of leafy branches the children had made to try to keep themselves separated from the other buzzing bugs and biting beasties that crawled and crept along the jungle floor.

'Bzzzrrrbzzzrrrbzzzrrrbzzzrrrbzzzrrrbzzzrrr…'

FIFTY

The Broken Cartwheel

'Tseeep!' 'Tseeep!' 'Tseeep!'

'Vvit!' 'Vvit!' 'Vvit!'

'Cheweeweewee!' 'Cheweeweewee!' 'Cheweeweewee!'

Tizzie rubbed her eyes as she awoke, once again, to the unmistakeable sounds of the Jungleland Dawn Chorus.

The exhausted young girl had hardly slept.

'Wakey, wakey, rise and WORK!' shouted Purgy.

'Gurrhhhh!'

Thwcrack!

Within minutes they were loaded down with their packs and marching out of camp in single file.

Lucy had to lead the zonkey pulling the barrel-cart. Since the tiny little girl was so sick, and so small, she wasn't much good at carrying anyway, so Purgy had assigned her to that job.

Lucy didn't really know where she was or what she should do. The big red lump on her arm from the giant mosquito bite had become much larger and more inflamed. Sweat was pouring from her skin. She was obviously confused.

'She's definitely got all the symptoms of airalam fever,' said Janxa with a worried look on her face.

Lucy was so sickly that it was almost inevitable she would do something wrong. After only a kilom or so, she led the zonkey right over a hole in the trail.

Splinkcrickcrack!

144

One of the cartwheels broke as it went down the hole.

It wasn't that big a hole. But the barrel was very heavy and the wheel just couldn't take the jolt.

Purgy hurried back along the trail to see what the problem was.

'Nohhhhhhh!'

He was beside himself with rage, pacing back and forwards with his palm on his forehead, as if frantically trying to decide what to do. The barrel was obviously very important.

Suddenly, Purgy stopped pacing and told some of the men and older boys to start unloading the huge container.

'We'll roll it,' he declared.

Having found a possible solution to his problem, he then turned and screamed at the top of his voice.

'GURT!!!'

As Pigleg's Punisher stepped forward with Lasher coiled in his hand, Purgy pointed his stubby finger at tiny, frail, sickly, little Lucy and passed sentence for her crime.

'TEN LASHES!'

Gurt always did as he was told.

And he loved lashing people.

Especially children, as they always screamed the loudest.

'Murmamurmamurma… bit harsh… murmamurmamurma…'

But there was a murmuring of dissension amongst the other men.

On hearing it, the heavily-tattooed pirate scanned his eyes from side to side, as if trying to gauge the mood of his shipmates.

'Errherrrrrr. Errherrrrrr. Errherrrrrr.'

Then he looked down at little Lucy as she sobbed.

She was only about six years old, and tiny for her age, and obviously very frail from her sickness.

'Murmamurmamurma… only a baby… murmamurmamurma…'

The muttering of the men got louder.

Tizzie could sense the tension.

Everyone knew who was in charge…

Purgy.

But everyone also knew that – sometimes – orders weren't followed if they went too far. If they crossed a line that not even a sea-hardened pirate would step over.

Then there would be mutiny.

Purgy waited, undecided.

Thud! Thud! Thud!

Gurt thudded forward.

A pirate gripped the handle of his dagger.

Suddenly, Purgy raised his hand to stop the punisher in his tracks.

'No lashing today. The girl's not well. Give her a shoulder ride.'

The murmuring amongst the men changed in tone. They all nodded vigorously and expressed their approval of Purgy's decision.

'A shoulder ride… murmamurmamurma… yeah, that's nice…'

'Gurrhhhh!'

Thwcrack!

Gurt, on the other hand, seemed to feel differently. He appeared to be genuinely disappointed by Purgy's change of mind. But he always did as he was told. Curling Lasher before putting the whip in his belt, he raised Lucy high into the air, dumped her onto his shoulders and began walking.

The heads of six of the older boys dropped as Purgy gave more orders. And with good reason.

For they now had back-breaking work to do.

They began *rolling* the huge barrel.

FIFTY-ONE

The Triple-Hoof

After a long morning of trudging, the jungle marchers suddenly reached the end of the South Trail.

Tizzie bumped into the child in front of her, as everybody came to an abrupt halt. Then she looked ahead.

A few steps further and there would be no canopy of branches and leaves above their heads, just an oasis of space in a desert of trees.

'Crosstrails Clearing at last,' said Purgy, telling everyone what they knew already. 'And in plenty of time to build the Cap'n's trap.'

The tattooed pirate then peered tentatively into the clearing.

'You first Baluta,' he said to one of the Saalung guides. 'You know what we're looking for. Muskets ready. Cover 'im, lads.'

Baluta moved forward, hesitantly, one small step at a time, scanning the ground for any signs of mutant wild boar. He appeared to be listening for the slightest sound that would signal an attack from the trees.

The musketmen aimed their guns into the clearing, ready to fire if called upon. But all seemed quiet. Baluta waved his arm and the others stepped, slowly and cautiously, into the clearing.

'Here,' said Baluta, pointing at the ground. 'Recent tracks... the triple-hoof.'

'Grunter,' mumbled Purgy.

'And another adult,' continued Baluta. 'And six boarlets... Yesterday.'

Purgy appeared to be delighted with that news.

'*Yesterday*… That means the pig is near, mates. Just what the Cap'n will want to hear.'

However, given everything they'd been told, it certainly wasn't what Tizzie and the other children wanted to hear. Nor, it appeared, did the other pirates relish the thought of Grunter being in the vicinity.

'But not too near just yet, eh Purgy?' joked one of the crew, scanning the clearing a little nervously.

'Aye,' replied the pudgy pirate, 'we certainly don't want to meet him before the Cap'n arrives and everything is in place.'

Then Purgy raised his voice a little to make sure that everyone could hear.

'And you'd do well to remember this…

'The Cap'n's orders are clear.

'It's he, and only he, among us, who will face that murderous boar.

'He has to be the one who finishes the beast.

'It's *his* revenge.'

FIFTY-TWO

The Cap'n's Trap

'Gurt, dump that girl and get those slaves working.'

Following Purgy's orders, Pigleg's punisher dumped little Lucy on the ground at the edge of the clearing and cracked Lasher three times to make sure the slaves were doing their jobs.

'Gurrhhhh!'

Thwcrack!

Lucy's sickness had clearly worsened. She tossed and turned and mumbled deliriously.

'No Mummy, I didn't do it… it wasn't me.'

'Airalam fever,' said Purgy as he spoke out loud to the other pirates, having just confirmed his diagnosis with a closer look at the huge red lump on Lucy's arm. 'We haven't got time for this. The Cap'n'll be here before long. We'll leave her there and let nature do its job. She'll be dead in a couple of days anyway.'

But, once again, Purgy only had to glance at the faces of the men under his command to know he had given the wrong order.

He quickly changed his mind and Janxa was given the job of preparing a medicine from the jungle plants.

Tizzie had learned that, once you had the fever, there was a very small likelihood of survival. But, if she had the medicine, at least Lucy would feel better for a litle while.

Tizzie, Jack, and the others were then forced to build what Purgy kept calling, 'the Cap'n's Trap'.

'Gurrhhhh!'

Thwcrack!

All the pirates and the Saalung had to help as the work required strong arms for sawing and axing and hammering.

'Gurrhhhh!'

Thwcrack!

There was frantic activity, with the children fetching and carrying and holding and pushing and pulling.

Some of the men built a wide platform set up high on long legs near the edge of the clearing.

Then the huge barrel was rolled and hauled and winched into position on top of the platform.

Meanwhile, Purgy supervised the children digging deep holes and setting snares made of nets and ropes.

In the middle of the clearing, eight posts were hammered into the ground in a circle, with each post opposite one of the trails that led into the jungle.

Then the other posts were hammered in at equal distances apart inside the circle of eight posts. A short length of rope was dropped down on the ground beside each post.

All the while, Tizzie was whispering with Jack and the others. They were trying to decide what each part of the trap was for and how it was going to work. They pretty much all agreed with Jack's assessment of the reason for the posts.

'We're going to be tied to them as bait when it comes to it.'

But none of them had come up with any idea as to what the barrel-on-the-platform arrangement was for.

Finally, the children got their answer.

Bnngg! Bnngg! Bnngg!

There were a few hollow bongs as a tap was hammered into place in the side of the barrel with a mallet.

Sqqkk!

Then there was a squeak as a pirate scaled the tower, stood on the platform, and turned on the tap.

'Oh yers.'

'Very good.'

'Yers.'

Whatever it was for, it apparently worked as planned, because there was then a lot of nodding and smiling and congratulating amongst the pirates.

Tizzie and the other children peered inquisitively over at the barrel to see what was coming out of the tap.

'Looks like peanut oil,' said Janxa. 'My mum uses it for cooking.'

'Right, that's the shower tower and everything else done,' said Purgy, looking at his list of instructions from Captain Pigleg for one final time. 'The Cap'n *has* to be pleased with our work today... we've completed every task he set, and done it all on time.'

As Purgy puffed himself up, the children whispered amongst themselves.

'Why would Pigleg want a peanut-oil shower built in the middle of the jungle?'

Janxa confirmed what they were all thinking.

'Whatever the reason, it probably won't be good for us.'

FIFTY-THREE

ONLY ME!!!

Captain Pigleg arrived at the Crosstrails Clearing in the late afternoon. He was accompanied by more pirates and more Saalung tribesmen.

'Well,' boomed Pigleg, 'let's see what you've done, then.'

Purgy took great delight in showing his master the Grunter traps and contraptions that had been constructed according to his instructions.

Tizzie watched as Pigleg first looked at and tested the traps and contraptions. Then he tested and looked at them again.

The pirate leader appeared to be very concerned that everything worked. He checked the poles that had been sunk into the ground, trying to move them to see if they would wobble.

He peered into the stake pit. Then he dropped a sack of salt onto one of the sharp stakes. The bag burst instantly as it hit the point of the stake and salt poured everywhere.

'Yaargghhh! That pit'll split a pig or two in two,' he growled menacingly, obviously very pleased with that particular trap.

Pigleg insisted on repeating the test twice more before a false top, camouflaged with branches and leaves, was placed over the pit.

'They'll never know it's there, Mr Cudgel,' said the Captain.

'A good trap, to be sure,' answered his first mate.

Captain Pigleg then insisted the snares were all tested.

The children had to take it in turns to step into the loops. When it came to Tizzie's turn, she had only just put her foot in the loop when the trap was sprung and it took her somewhat by surprise.

'Eeeeeeeeeeeeeeeeeee!'

She screamed as she was carried up into the air by one leg and left dangling there for what seemed like ages until they got her down.

'YAYYY!'

Pigleg and the other pirates roared their delight every time one of the children flew upwards.

By early evening, as it began to get darker in the clearing, the Captain seemed satisfied that his traps and contraptions were ready.

'Just one last check,' he said, as he tested the biggest contraption again.

'He must have tested that tower shower ten times,' said Jack.

'What *is* it for?' wondered Janxa.

Pigleg then stood on an upturned wooden tub to tell the men his plan.

'It'll be dusk soon. Grunter's main huntin' time. This is our best chance to lure him to the clearing. I want a volunteer to go down each trail for one thousand paces and scatter peanuts on the ground all the way from here to there.

'You, you, you, you, you, you, you, and you.'

After the Captain had chosen the eight 'volunteers', each man was handed a large sack of peanuts which he put over his shoulder in readiness to leave.

But before the men set out on their dangerous mission, Pigleg spoke to all his crew again in a very serious warning tone.

'I'm bettin' Grunter won't be able to resist the peanut trails that these brave mates are going to lay. And when he gets here, to Crosstrails Clearing, this thing is going to end. Right here, right then.

'One way or another, it'll be the finish of it.

'It'll be Sweet Revenge for me...

'Or... the big pig...'

At that moment, Pigleg stretched to open up the long wooden box that was being offered to him at arms length by Purgy.

A hush came over the clearing as those present contemplated the imminent battle in silence.

Then Pigleg began rousing his men with fighting talk.

'But I'm bettin' it'll be me that's still standin', lads.'

'Coz I'm going to introduce Grunter to my new friend...

'BLUNDER... BESS!

'You've all heard her shout, mates!'

'Aye, Cap'n!' agreed the men in unison as Pigleg continued.

'She's a match for any mutant pigcreature, I'd wager.

'Aye, Cap'n!' agreed the men again.

'Now, before we go any further...

'I want everyone here to remember one thing...

'I've waited oohh soohh long for my *revenge*...

'Too long to have its sweet taste spoiled...

'So, no matter how close that big mutant pig gets to me...

'No matter how much it looks like he's going to chew me up...

'No matter how bad it looks...

'It's *only me* who can *kill* that boar...

'Do ya *hear*?!

'ONLY ME!!!'

FIFTY-FOUR

Sticky Showers

'Aye, aye, Cap'n,' said the pirates in unison, to show they agreed it would only be him who could finish off Grunter.

Pigleg stepped off the upturned tub, and it was placed, the right way up, directly beneath the barrel tap.

As the eight unlucky men who had been volunteered set off down the paths from the clearing in order to lay the peanut trails, the children were made to stand in line near the shower tower.

'Right, shower time,' said Purgy.

'Oh no, it's for us!' moaned Janxa as she lined up with the others. 'We're going to get covered in oil.'

'They'll reek of peanuts!' said Pigleg gleefully. 'That'll make 'em seem like an even tastier little snack for Grunter, eh mates?'

'Aye, Cap'n,' said all the pirates, with almost equal glee.

It was soon Tizzie's turn. She walked forward and stepped into the wooden tub.

Purgy pulled the lever. Sticky peanut oil was released. A big dollop of the yellowy, treacly liquid poured down onto the top of her head in one sticky splodge. Purgy turned the tap off.

'Eeeehhh!'

Tizzie squeaked and wriggled and squirmed as the oil dripped down all over her; first down over her ears and face and neck, and then down over her back and front and arms.

'Stand still,' ordered Purgy.

'Gurrhhhh!'

Thwcrack!

Tizzie forced herself to do as she was told as the oil trickled down her legs and collected around her toes in the tub.

'Keep 'em movin', Mr Cudgel,' said Pigleg. 'It's getting darker, and the big pig'll be a huntin' soon.'

'Purgy, you heard the Cap'n.'

'Out then, hurry, hurry,' chivvied Purgy.

Tizzie jumped from the tub and stood with the five others who were already covered in oil. Like them, her hair was all straggly. She looked and felt miserable.

After ten children had had their oily shower, four of the pirates took the tub and poured the surplus oil back into the barrel at the top.

'That's it, mates, pour it in carefully,' said Pigleg. 'Don't want to waste any.'

Streaks of sticky oil ran down Tizzie's arms and legs whilst she stood still, wondering what horror would come next.

'Salt 'em, mates,' said Pigleg, 'we know the pig loves 'is chop nice and salty.'

'That he does, Cap'n, that he does,' agreed Cudgel. 'Purgy, you heard the Cap'n.'

Mr Purgy had already put three sticks flat on the ground, end to end in a line. He and two other pirates picked up a bag of salt each. They untied the strings. Each of the three pirates then stood behind one of the sticks, facing the children.

'Right, you lot, come and get it, three at a time.'

Tizzie moved towards one of the three sticks, with Jack and Janxa accompanying her. When she got to the stick, she stopped as instructed.

Purgy poured the bag of salt over her head, shaking it

afterwards to make sure that every last bit of salt came out. It was horrible, all gritty and grainy. It made her skin itch.

Jack and Janxa received the same salty shower.

'Right, back in line,' barked Purgy. 'Next three.'

After all the children had been oiled and salted, Pigleg seemed well satisfied as he surveyed his bait.

'Arrgghhhh. Peanut-flavoured childflesh...

'Grunter won't be able to able to resist ye!'

FIFTY-FIVE

The Oinkroar

Suddenly, a terrifying sound made Tizzie jump out of her skin.

'OIOIAUROIOIAUROIOIAURRRRRRR!'

'The oinkroar,' said Janxa, her voice trembling.

Pigleg whispered under his breath.

'He's close.'

'Nohhhhhhhhhhhhhhhhhhhhhhhhhhhhhhhhh!

'Aaaaaaaaaaaaaaaaaaarrrrrrrrrrrrrrrrggggggggggghhhhhhhhhhhhhh!'

Tizzie looked at Jack as she heard the terrifying sound of a man screaming for mercy in the distance.

'OIOIAUROIOIAUROIOIAURRRRRRR!'

This time it seemed as if Grunter's roar had tunnelled down the North Trail and burst out into the clearing.

'Nohhhhhhhhhhhhhhhhhhhhhh.

'Aaaaarrrrrrrrrrrrrrrggggggggghhhhh!'

The man screamed again in the distance.

'He's eating him,' murmured Janxa.

'He starts with the feet,' said Yang, but without his usual enthusiasm. Perhaps he understood that real people were really dying. And it could be him next.

'Nohhhhhhhhhhhhhhh.

'Aaaaarrrrrrrrrrggggggghhhh!'

Tizzie covered her ears. She didn't want to listen.

'Get the traps ready… NOW!' bawled Pigleg. 'He'll be comin' fer us soon enough.'

'Nohhhhh!

'Aaaarrrrrrrrrrgggggghhh!'

At intervals, they heard the sound of pleading and screaming and crying as the unfortunate pirate was being eaten alive – slowly but surely – by Big Red Grunter.

Just then, all seven of the other pirates scampered back into the clearing from each of the other trails, their faces white with fear.

'Nohhh!

'Aaaaarrrrrggghhh!'

'Oh, for pity's sake, finish it quickly,' murmured Cudgel, as he listened to his shipmate's scream.

Now even some of the pirates covered their ears. This all seemed to be too much to bear, even for the toughest of them. Except Pigleg, who was so focused on the task at hand that he appeared to be completely insensitive to the plight of his crewman.

'Put the 'E' graders on the outside,' he ordered, with an air of grim determination.

The seven children who got 'E' at the Sandland Slave School were quickly tied to the outer ring of posts with ropes.

Jack whispered to Tizzie.

'They're going to be first in line to be eaten by Grunter.'

'One post spare, Cap'n,' said Purgy, nodding in Tizzie's direction as he did so.

'Ah, yes, Little Miss Troublemouth,' said Pigleg. 'Put 'er on it.'

The tattoo-mouth grinned its widest grin.

Tizzie wriggled and writhed, but Purgy was far too strong and she soon found herself tied to the post opposite the North Trail exit.

But it's just not *fair*, thought the indignant young girl.

I got a 'B'.

FIFTY-SIX

Pig Chop

Once the rest of the children had been tied to the inner posts, Pigleg shouted a strange order...

'Pile the peanuts!'

There was now frantic activity amongst the pirates. They grabbed up the sacks, slit them open with their knives, and poured a pile of peanuts onto the ground around the legs of each child.

Purgy poured from a sack in front of Tizzie. The tattoo-mouth grinned wildly and his eyes were full of glee as he repeated a phrase he'd thought of over and over.

'Little Miss Pig Chop soon... Little Miss Pig Chop soon... Little Miss Pig Chop soon...'

Tizzie felt the patter of peanuts on the top of her feet. The shells tickled her legs as the pile rose up around her. She was soon standing in a pyramid of peanuts right up to her knees.

A shiver of fear went down Tizzie's spine as she realised that this could be the end of her short life.

She could soon be eaten slowly, from the feet up, by a big pig with razor sharp teeth.

The frightened young girl began to tremble at just the thought of it.

'Now there's chop fit for a pig!' grinned Pigleg, as he surveyed all the children tied to posts – his living, breathing bait – with great satisfaction.

'OIOIAUROIOIAUROIOIAURRRRRRR!'

The oinkroar was louder still.

Grunter was now *very* close.

'He's here!' bawled Pigleg.

'Bring me me Thunder Gun!'

A trembling pirate obliged.

Clish, thud, Clish, thud, Clish, thud.

Pigleg paced purposefully over to stand right in front of Tizzie, his hoof sounding very different on the jungle floor than it did on the deck of the ship.

The pirate captain raised Blunder Bess and aimed it down the North Trail as his hair first glowed... and then ignited.

In a moment of spontaneous combustion, his whole head was afire. As his hair blazed, Pigleg screamed dementedly at the top of his voice.

'I'M READY FOR YE, GRUNTER!'

Tizzie strained her neck to look around Pigleg's freakish flaming form.

Grunter was thundering down the trail, heading straight towards them, creating a puffing cloud of dust and stones in his wake.

The beast was like no other pig or boar she had ever seen.

It was a mud-red-brown.

It was covered in blood-stained, dirt-matted hair.

It had four huge pointed tusks.

Its jaws were open wide, baring two rows of razorteeth.

The tusks and teeth were dripping with fresh, warm blood.

The hairy mutant monster roared again as it entered the clearing.

'OIOIAUROIOIAUROIOIAURRRRRRR!'

FIFTY-SEVEN

Attack Of The Boarmonsters

'OIOIAUROIOIAUROIOIAURRRRRRR!'

Grunter charged straight at Pigleg.

His eyes blazed with hatred.

Tizzie trembled as the ground shook.

'OIOIAUROIOIAURRRRRRRR!'

Now Saowa roared as she entered the clearing from the South Trail.

'Another boar!'

A command from Cudgel.

'Muskets and spears ready!'

'Oioiaurrrrrrrrrrr!'

'Oioiaurrrrrrrrrrr!'

'Oioiaurrrrrrrrrrr!'

'Oioiaurrrrrrrrrrr!'

'Oioiaurrrrrrrrrrr!'

'Oioiaurrrrrrrrrrr!'

'More boars!'

The six boarlets each roared loudly as they entered the clearing from the other six trails.

'Six more!'

'Fire at will!'

Tizzie glanced across at Grunter's offspring.

They were like small versions of their father.

But 'small' was only a relative term.

Each was far bigger than a lion! They were *all* monsters.

The coordinated attack of the Grunters was so unexpected that it threw the pirates and the Saalung into disarray.

'Every man for himself!'

'Oioiaurrrrrrrrrrr!'

Fzzzzzzzzzzzzzz. Pshhhhhhhhh. Weeeeeeeeee.

'Oioiaurrrrrrrrrrr!'

Fzzzzzzzzzzzzzz. Pshhhhhhhhh. Weeeeeeeeee.

The boarbeasts charged.

The men fired their muskets and bows.

And threw their spears.

Pigleg was momentarily distracted by all the commotion.

'OIOIAUROIOIAUROIOIAURRRRRRR!'

But he quickly came to his senses just in time when Grunter roared again.

The fearless pirate aimed Blunder Bess… and fired.

THUBOOOOOOOOOMMMMMMMMMMMMMM!!!

Piff! Thuff! Piff! Thuff!

The thundershot ripped into Grunter's flesh.

'Squeeeeeeeeeeeeeeeeeeee!'

The huge boarmonster squealed and staggered.

And slowed momentarily.

But he was a pigcreature possessed.

'OIOIAUROIOIAUROIOIAURRRRRRR!'

And he just kept on coming with his roaring jaws open wide.

Pigleg put up his hook arm to protect himself from the razor-teeth.

Clsshh!

He just managed to draw his cutlass as the boar fell on him.

Clink!

Grunter bit down hard on the golden hook.

Rrripp!

With one twist of his head and neck, he tore the hook from Pigleg's arm.

Spttt!

The boarmonster spat out the hook.

Pigleg saw his chance and swung his cutlass.

Slshhh!

The cutlass swiped into the flesh of Grunter's neck.

Khhh!

Until it hit bone.

'Squeeeeeeeeeeeeeeeeeeee!'

Blood spurted and gushed from the wound.

But the boar still wasn't finished.

It bit again.

This time locking its jaws around Pigleg's pegleg.

Its own severed leg bone.

'Naarrggghhhh!'

Pigleg drew back his cutlass for another swipe at the beast's hairy neck.

Rrripp!

Grunter twisted his head again, ripping the pegleg right out from under the Captain.

'Aaaarrrrggggghhhhhhhhhh!'

The toughest pirate who had ever lived fell to the ground, dropping his weapon as he put out his hand to break his fall.

'OIOIAUROIOIAUROIOIAURRRRRRR!'

The most ferocious boarmonster who had ever lived spat out the leg bone and roared triumphantly for the whole jungle to hear as he turned to finish off his prey.

'Nohhhhhhhhhhhhhhhhhhhhhhhhhhhhhhhhhhh!'

Tizzie screamed in fear.

She knew she would be next.

'OIOIAUROIOIAUROIOIAURRRRRRR!'

Grunter roared and stared at Tizzie, momentarily distracted by her scream.

Squelch!

'Squeeee!'

Grunter squealed a small squeal of surprise.

Pigleg had seized his chance.

And struck a blow with his dagger.

Deep into the pig's underbelly.

He had punctured the monster's heart.

The giant chewing creature was dead before it hit the jungle floor.

With a dull heavy thud.

Thubbbbbbbbbbbbbbbbb!

FIFTY-EIGHT

Chaos In The Clearing

'OIOIAUROIOIAURRRRRRRR!'

   'Oioiaurrrrrrrrrr!'

   'Oioiaurrrrrrrrrr!'

   'Oioiaurrrrrrrrrr!'

   'Oioiaurrrrrrrrrr!'

   'Oioiaurrrrrrrrrr!'

   'Oioiaurrrrrrrrrr!'

There was chaos in the clearing as the boarmonsters careered around in all directions, roaring and biting and chewing and roaring.

Seven men were already dead.

'Helllp mee...'

'Helllllllllllp, pleassse...'

'Helllllllp meee...'

Eleven more lay wounded.

Screaming for help.

One boarlet was dying on the ground, panting heavily, a spear stuck in its flank.

Another boarlet had fallen down a stake pit.

'Squee!'

It was killed the instant it landed on the sharp spikes at the bottom.

'Oioiaurrrrrrrrrr!'

Yet another roared its frustration, kicking and wriggling as it dangled helplessly in the air inside a netsnare.

'OIOIAUROIOIAURRRRRRRR!'

Hzzzzzzzzzzzzz. Pshhhhhhhh. Weeeeeeeee.

'Oioiaurrrrrrrrrrr!'

Hzzzzzzzzzzzzz. Pshhhhhhhh. Weeeeeeeee.

'Oioiaurrrrrrrrrrr!'

Hzzzzzzzzzzzzz. Pshhhhhhhh. Weeeeeeeee.

'Oioiaurrrrrrrrrrr!'

Hzzzzzzzzzzzzz. Pshhhhhhhh. Weeeeeeeee.

Oioiaurrrrrrrrrrr!'

Hzzzzzzzzzzzzz. Pshhhhhhhh. Weeeeeeeee.

Saowa and her remaining offspring roared and bit and chewed with increasing ferocity as they tore around the clearing.

Leaves, mud, dust, and stones flew everywhere.

The pirates and Saalung responded as best they could, discharging their weapons in every direction as they desperately tried to defend themselves against the attack of the boarmonsters.

Tizzie struggled to free herself from the ropes tying her to the post.

Her end looked inevitable.

The men would soon be defeated.

Then the boars would eat the peanut-flavoured children.

From the toes up.

Slowly.

Tizzie wriggled and struggled harder.

But, try as she might, she couldn't even loosen the ropes that bound her.

'OIOIAUROIOIAURRRRRRRR!'

The inevitable had come even quicker than Tizzie had imagined.

'OIOIAUROIOIAURRRRRRRR!'

Saowa had broken off from the fighting.

And was now roaring.

And salivating.

Only a few feet in front of the terrified young girl.

'OIOIAUROIOIAURRRRRRRR!'

Grunter's mate roared again loudly…

As she made ready to feast on peanut-flavoured childflesh.

Tizzie screamed and strained against her bonds.

'Hellllllllllllllllpppppppppppp!'

Jack saw the danger.

But he was powerless to help his friend.

All he could manage was a feeble cry from behind her.

'Nohhhhhhhhhhhhhhhhhhhhh!

'Not Tizzieeee.'

FIFTY-NINE

GET THAT BOYYY!

Saowa took another salivating step towards Tizzie.

The boarmonster opened her huge jaws to take the first bite with her razorteeth.

Only two more steps…

And it was going to *hurt*.

A *lot*.

'TIZZIE!'

At that precise moment, the terrified young girl heard an unexpected but very familiar voice through all the other noise.

No it *can't* be, she thought.

How could *he* be *here*?

There was suddenly even greater pandemonium in the Crosstrails Clearing.

THUBOOOOOOOOOMMMMMMMMMMMMMMM!!!

Piff! Thuff! Piff! Thuff!

The thundershot from Blunder Bess ripped into Saowa's flesh right before Tizzie's eyes.

'Squeeeeeeeeeeeeeeeeeeee!'

The boarmonster fell dead at Tizzie's feet before it could take one bite.

Psssshhhh!

Its head crashed into the pile of peanuts with a pishing sound.

Pigleg yelled.

'Yaarrrrrrrrggggggggggghhhhhhhhhhhhhh!'

Tizzie looked over at him.

He was standing in the pose of a triumphant trophy hunter.

He had retrieved his hook and his pegleg.

And he now stood proud, with his right foot on the ground and his hoof resting on Grunter's corpse; his weapon of choice in his hand.

Hzzzzzzzzzzzzz.

Pshhhhhhhhh.

Fweeeeeeeeee.

Boooom.

Now the Bulubaa attacked from the trees with all the weapons at their disposal.

They had just arrived.

And immediately saw the danger in the clearing.

They were desperate to save their children from slavery… and, more pressingly, the boarmonsters.

Kzzzzzzzzzzzzzzzzzzzzz.

Princess Kea, who had been hiding and watching in the trees, fired her Kernbow.

'Squeeeeeeeeeeeeeeeeeeeeee!'

A boarmonster fell.

Cabooom! Foooom!

Clevercloggs deployed two cleversticks in quick succession, taking out two groups of heavily armed Saalung.

Mzzzzzzzzzzzzzzzzzzz!

Mr Sand, a crack-shot and former sniper instructor, gave musket fire from a concealed position in the trees.

'TIZZIE!!!'

Louis called his sister's name again.

He had also just arrived moments earlier.

Seeing his sister in mortal danger, he quickly unsheathed his Kaski and pulled out the sharp blade.

He ran into the clearing behind Hans, who held two blazing pistols.

Tizzie screamed with joy.

'LOUIS!!!'

The brave young boy ran towards his sister.

'TIZZIE!!!'

He was *soooh* happy to see her.

'LOUIS!!!'

She was *soooh* happy to see him.

Hans ran towards Lucy.

She was very sick, but she remembered his promise from all that time ago in the hold.

'Vee vill look after you, Lucy.'

Hans picked up the tiny girl in his arms and moved her away from the chaos in the clearing and deeper into the trees.

'You'll be safer here, little one. I vill be back for you soon.'

With that, he hurriedly returned to the clearing to help the others.

Meanwhile, the Bulubaa and the rescuers fought the Saluung and the pirates.

And everyone fought the boarmonsters.

As the battle in the clearing raged, Louis hurriedly cut Tizzie from the post with his knife before moving on to free the child on the next post.

Hans ran to the posts and did the same.

Within minutes, all the children had been cut free.

Suddenly, there was a bellow that could be heard above all the other noise in the clearing.

'GUUURRRRTTTT!

'GET THAT BOYYY!'

Pigleg had recognised Louis from the 'Wanted' poster.

Tizzie could see over Louis' shoulder that the pirate captain was pointing at her brother with his hook.

'They're after *you*, Louis.

'This way.'

With that, she took Louis' hand, turned, and ran towards one of the paths, pulling Louis along behind.

'Gurrrrhhhhhhhhhh!'

As Louis was pulled along by Tizzie, he heard Gurt gurgle behind him.

Thwcrack!

He felt Lasher bite as the whip wrapped itself around his ankle.

It held and tripped him at the same time, stopping him abruptly in his tracks.

His hand was wrenched from Tizzie's as he fell.

Tizzie tripped and fell too.

Next second, Louis was being dragged along the ground.

Away from his sister.

He dug his fingers in.

It was a desperate attempt to save himself, just as he had done when Monstro attacked him.

'LOUIS!!! NOOHHHH!!!'

He could hear Tizzie's desperate cry as she was pulled away towards safety by one of the Bulubaa warriors.

Tizzie tripped and fell again.

'Run girl… this way, into the trees,' shouted the man, as he ducked and darted to avoid the bullets and spears and arrows that were whizzing around the clearing.

Louis struggled.

If he could just remove the whip from his ankle, he may be able to catch Tizzie up.

He reached for his catapult and managed to pull it out.

Stmppp!

A heavy hoof trod down on his wrist, preventing him from using his weapon.

Pigleg looked down on him with a mixture of menace and contempt.

'You'll not be killin' me today, assassin boy!

'Back to the ship, lads.

'Leave the other slaves.

'This one's all we need.'

SIXTY

A Horrible Way To Die

Despite the chaos and danger in the clearing, all Tizzie could think about was Louis.

She jumped to her feet and started to run back to him.

Boom!

An explosion right in front of her made her stop running.

'LOUIS!!!'

Then, screaming as she watched her little brother being carried away under Gurt's arm, she was suddenly aware of danger from above.

She looked up, and could only watch in horror, rooted to the spot by what she saw.

A hoard of tree octopuses was gliding silently down.

They were like hairy parachutes descending from the canopy.

Their beaks were open wide.

Tizzie couldn't move.

The hairy creatures fell on all her friends and foes alike.

'Ahrhhmmm…'

'Urghhhhmmm…'

'Ehrhhmmm…'

Everyone's screams were muffled as the armtentacles of the octopuses enfolded them.

Jack managed to point and shout before his mouth was covered.

'LOOK OUT, TIZZmmm…'

The terrified young girl looked up to where Jack had pointed.

A tree octopus was only feet above her, its hairy armtentacles and rubbery body outstretched as it attacked.

She had no time to react.

The creature landed on her, its hard beak banging against her head as it did so.

'Helmmm…'

Her scream for help was muffled by one of the monster's suckers covering her mouth as it pulled her to the ground.

The tree octopus wound its armtentacles in a tighter and tighter grip around her whole body.

She was totally unable to move.

As it opened its beak to take the first bite, all Tizzie could think of was what Yang had said about the attack of this gruesome predator…

'*It's a horrible way to die.*'

- NEXT -

After reading *Pigleg's Revenge*, the fourth book in the Kernowland series, you may want certain questions answered:

Will Tizzie die horribly in the clutches of the hairy tree octopus?

Will Louis be taken back to Wonrekland by Captain Pigleg and executed with the Guillotine of Sirap?

Will the sacked teachers have their heads chopped off with the guillotine too?

What will the heroic rescuers – Princess Kea, Mr Sand, Clevercloggs, and Misty – do now?

How will the parents make Lister's Choice?

What will it be like in Wonrekland for the one child from each family who is sold into slavery?

Will Cule, Bella, and the Guardians of Kernow, find sanctuary and assistance in Acirema North?

What and where are Godolphin's *Amulet of Hope* and *Photos* the *Crystal of Light*?

If so, you may get some answers by reading *Book 5* in the Kernowland series:

Slavechildren

Visit our websites for up-to-date information

www.kernowland.com
www.erthwurld.com

ERTH

GLACIERLAND

E

SNC

WILDLAND

E

ACIREMA NORTH

The Revenger

PRARIELAND

LAKELAND

E

Ratlarbig Rock

Port of Acnalbasac

Isles of Airanac

CIFICAP OCEAN

QUAKELAND

SWAMPLAND

Abuc

Tizzie

De

CAVELAND

Port Lujnab

E

CITNALTA OCEAN

RIVERLAND

ACIREMA SOUTH

E

MOUNTAINLAND

Cap'n Pigleg of The Revenger

N

W   E

S

NREHTUOS OC

E